AN
IMPROBABLE
SPY

AN IMPROBABLE SPY

DAVID PAUL COLLINS

iUniverse®

AN IMPROBABLE SPY

iUniverse books may be ordered through booksellers or by contacting:

iUniverse
1663 Liberty Drive
Bloomington, IN 47403
www.iuniverse.com
1-800-Authors (1-800-288-4677)

Map Illustration	Tim Barker
Website	Darlene Brice
Author Photo	Unknown

ISBN: 978-1-5320-8010-4 (sc)
ISBN: 978-1-5320-8030-2 (e)

Library of Congress Control Number: 2019913295

Print information available on the last page.

iUniverse rev. date: 09/19/2019

To my amazing wife, Victoria.
From a man you never knew.

When you have eliminated the impossible,
whatever remains,
however improbable,
must be the truth.

—Sherlock Holmes, in *The Sign of the Four* by
Sir Arthur Conan Doyle

CONTENTS

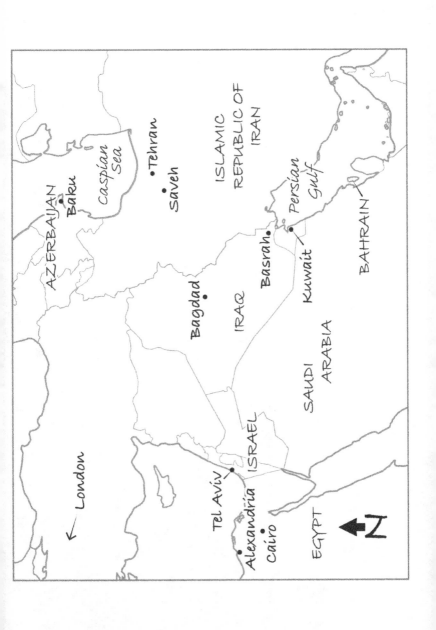

ONE

Moscow, March 1980

Subzero temperatures did not make Vladimir Sudakov shiver as he walked down Vasilyevskaya Street among the crush of office workers hurrying to the metro. The sight of a coworker—a former Stasi officer—did. Stefan Kantwasser's penchant for not covering his Nordic blond hair with a *ushanke* cap made him easy to spot. When they had left their desks in the Office of the Chief Translator a half hour earlier, Kantwasser said he was on the way to meet a date for the Bolshoi Theater. It was in the opposite direction. Shaken, Sudakov slowed his steps, lengthening the distance between them.

The Stasi turned into the corner flower shop, easing Sudakov's fear that he was being shadowed. *A lady always appreciates flowers.* Sudakov shouldered into the wind, continuing his walk of no return, relegating the Stasi sighting to coincidence. Then he saw him again. As Sudakov walked by the taxi rank at the metro's exit, he saw the Stasi get into a black cab. He was not carrying flowers. Sudakov backed into a doorway, slinking low into his greatcoat, watching the cab drive away. He was sure that Kantwasser was staring through the frosted window directly at him.

Sudakov's heart pounded as he tried to rationalize why the German was so far away from his engagement. If

Kantwasser was tracking him, and if he had found out about Sudakov's plans, the timetable would have to be moved up—quickly. He turned toward the metro, stepping up his pace as fellow Muscovites hurried past him to their evening trains deep inside the Barrikadnaya subway station. He brushed through the crowds, trying to stay calm. He knew his next step was irreversible; his life would change forever. Under the reflected glare from a montage of small tiles, an abstraction of Vladimir Illych Lenin towered to the ceiling of the central platform. The tiles were set so that Lenin's image followed each person who looked at him. Sudakov looked away. He was about to betray Lenin; the USSR; his family, friends, and comrades; and the KGB.

Sudakov shuddered, thinking about being seen on a metro platform where he had no business. He looked left, right, up, down in a practiced movement without moving his head, worrying about a tail. He had rehearsed the plan in other metro stations, having convinced himself there was no other way. If he was caught, the note he palmed would be his death certificate.

Justification played like a favorite song in his mind. He hated the USSR for its ruthless slaughter of citizens like his grandfather in the Magadan gulags. Promotions had been denied by spiteful bosses with no explanation, and he detested his wife, who kept a long list of his shortcomings. But life in America would be different. He would be rewarded when the US learned what the Russians were doing in Iran, when they made the connection that his Middle East section comrades were persuading Ayatollah Khomeini's Revolutionary Guard to pull the American hostages out of their embassy's cellar and then hide them in six different locations—some in the Dasht-e Kavir Desert, some on the border with Azerbaijan.

Excitement and terror coursing through his body, Sudakov stole a glance at Lenin, who continued to keep his eyes fixed on him. He scanned the crowd. Paranoia kept him alert.

In the dull routine in drafty KGB offices, Sudakov had carried out boring assignments day after day, studying notes and photographs of foreign diplomats who had been identified as spies. American CIA officers were his targets, waiting to be uncovered in dossiers about newcomers joining their embassy. Sudakov's training at the Institute of International Relations gave him superior skills as a translator, which landed him a prized job concentrating on the bona fides of Americans on their ambassador's staff— usually CIA operatives. One stood out; he was listed as a defense analyst. In reality, he was the number-two CIA man in the USSR. Sudakov had shadowed him for days, learning his routine.

In the cold, musty station, Sudakov spotted the man walking with the controlled confidence he envied in Americans. The target—a tall, slender, bookish man—was familiar.

Glancing at his government-issued steel watch, he noted he had one minute and thirty seconds until the American's train for Kuznetsky Station would arrive. The man continued to his usual spot on the tiled subway platform, lingering at the back of the crowd. His face was thin with a sturdy jaw and high cheekbones. Traces of gray were set against a full head of wavy black hair that had been ribbed by a wide-tooth comb. His eyes focused straight ahead, feigning oblivion. He carried the day's *Pravda*—Cyrillic edition.

Sudakov envied CIA agents for looking cool, as they called it, while they outmaneuvered the KGB. His aspirations to become a "cool" senior KGB agent were always quashed by the bosses. "You are a nobody," they had said. "You will never be promoted. You're an imbecile." Americans were smarter than Russians; they would welcome him like a hero—an important KGB agent who would be appreciated for obtaining deep, dark secrets. He knew he was smart.

His aspiration of freedom came into focus when the American got closer. The man was enviably dressed, wearing an impeccably tailored dark blue suit, a regimental red-and-gold-striped tie knotted snugly on his white button-down shirt. Sudakov could see himself dressing just like that. Oblivious to the chill in the depths of the station, the agent had his topcoat resting on his arm, his narrow black shoes buffed to a luster that reflected the ceiling lights. Sudakov glanced down at his own shoes and frowned. They were dull, shabby, thick soled—more like boots. The rumpled black suit he wore was exactly like the brown one on a hook in his closet. Tens of thousands of identical suits, fabricated by the Novgorod Textile Factory and stamped for government use, clothed KGB agents around the world. Sudakov concluded in his youth, during his Komsomol training, that he would always be stuck with whatever the Soviet government decided its agents would wear. Choice was a matter for bosses of the evolving proletariat only.

Sudakov knew the American's expression would not change when he approached, so he sucked in his fat cheeks, ignored a knot in his belly, and moved toward his target. He had to move quickly; in thirty seconds the train would arrive. The note in his hand felt like a time bomb; he still had time to turn and walk away before his bomb exploded. He shook off the thought and moved into the crowd.

Sudakov watched the agent tuck the newspaper under his arm. The moment had come. He sidled next to the American, brushing his elbow into the target's side. "Take this," he said in thick, accented English, passing the handwritten note as if it were an invitation to a party.

> Middle East Unit advising Iran to
> disburse American hostages.
> Sunday, Slovetsky Park by obelisk.
> Send someone. 3.00 p.m.
> V. Sudakov, MEU

The American did not look at the note. He crushed it in his pocket and stepped forward to his train, just another commuter.

Sudakov joined the masses exiting up the stairs. He took a last look at the rear of the departing train; its roar trailed off as the last of its shiny silver cars disappeared into the orifice toward Kuznetsky Station. Sudakov trembled. The borders between the East and the West are separated by a no-man's-land, and he was in it.

Slovetsky Park's signature obelisk soared through a crescent of trees at the end of a broad walkway to a raised wooden bandstand. Musicians wrinkled their olive uniforms while climbing the platform steps, dragging assorted instruments, grumbling about the sad life of a third-rate musician. A firebird on the patent-leather bill of an officer's cap identified the maestro; a thick baton was clutched irreverently in his tight fist. In front of the bandstand, curved benches on either side of the walkway began to fill with Russian grandmothers, a few planting restless grandchildren at their sides. Aging babushkas outnumbered lonely old men on the benches ten to one. Slovetsky Park's musicians took their seats, beat their drums, squealed their bows, and bleated their horns. The first concert of spring was about to begin.

Sudakov studied the crowd and chose a seat in the back row of benches with a clear view of the park. Halfway through the first movement of Mussorgsky's "Night on Bald Mountain," his target approached the far side of the crescent. The American, walking a dog, feigned interest in the music as he strode past the obelisk.

The satisfaction Sudakov had felt that the next leg of his plan was on track evaporated when a demon rose in his troubled brain to ask, *What if the man is actually a KGB double agent?* His eyes darted over the crowd, searching for someone trailing the American. Everyone in the USSR watched everyone else.

Stupid mind, stupid mind, he chastised himself. Self-doubt defined him; confidence was never a strong trait. Sudakov turned slightly, indicating the man with the dog was welcome to choose his bench. Pleasant greetings would not be exchanged in the life-and-death reality of the moment.

When the American got settled, Sudakov reached out a perspiring hand to pat the dog. He spoke in a thick whisper that increased in volume as the percussionists thundered the storm on the mountain. "I am Middle East specialist.

Speak Arabic. Leave to Cairo tonight. Hate KGB, hate stupid Soviet Union, love America. KGB making deals in Iran to hurt your side. Hostages will die." He bent to tie his shoe and pulled an arch-shaped bracelet off his leg. "Here is microfiche. Your side need it. Contact me in Cairo."

The American took the bracelet, reached over the dog, and placed it on his ankle. "Bar, Semiramis Hotel, Cairo. Three o'clock, one week from today," said the American. "If this stuff is any good, there will be a man waiting for you, playing with his ring."

The dog pulled on his leash and made clear it was time to water the trees. In the hedge at the side of the bandstand, a landscape artist had trimmed an image of Lenin in the leafy green bushes. A smile crossed Sudakov's face as the band played a coda and the dog headed for Lenin.

TWO

Ladbroke's Hotel, London, Two Months Earlier

Within an hour of landing at Heathrow from Kuwait, Jack Devlin checked into Ladbroke's Belgravia Hotel—his favorite. He loved the perks of his merchant banking business: staying in the best hotels, dining in five-star restaurants, and entertaining lovelies until something came up. Sometimes it was the sun.

Harry, the concierge, caught Jack at the elevator and handed him a note. "Mornin' gov'nor, welcome back. Ya had a visitor, just missed him. Big, tough-looking black bloke. Left this; said it was confidential." Harry cupped his hands and whispered, "Secret."

Alone in the elevator, Jack opened the envelope, read the note, shook his head, and read it again.

> Jack,
>
> Hope this note finds you well. I am in London on business and learned our dates matched. I'll come by for breakfast tomorrow at nine.
>
> Hugh Ebanks
> 7 January

Life's turns and twists had amazed Jack in the past, but never like this. It was unfathomable how someone he had gone to sea with twenty years earlier knew he would be in London, staying at Ladbroke's. He and Hugh had exchanged occasional holiday cards but had not talked since their adventures in the brawling, wild ports of South America. Both had loved the barroom brawls, fights with cops, and run-ins with gangs of locals in which they had traded blows until just two men were left standing—Jack Devlin and Hugh Ebanks. Or, on a particularly bad night, just Hugh Ebanks.

Jack unlocked the door to his room, dropped his suitcase, and sat on the edge of the bed. Famished, he ordered room service and then read the note a second time, surprised that an old friend had gone to such trouble to get together.

The gray lethargy of a sleepless night gave way to a gray morning of heavy rain. Jack crawled out of bed, stumbled to the bathroom, and turned on the shower, full force and cold. He dressed in his usual three-piece suit, rescheduled his early-morning calls, and ran down the stairs to the lobby.

January of 1980 was predicted to be the coldest, rainiest, and darkest month London had seen in years. One glance through the lobby window confirmed the awful weather had already set in. Breakfast guests crowded the room, lingering over tea before braving the storm. For Jack, the London weather would not be a problem for long. A few shivering days, then he would be back in the sunshine of Kuwait and his struggling merchant banking business.

A gust of wind blew the street-side door open in a test of its brass hinges and brought Hugh Ebanks into the dining room so suddenly Jack felt as though he had been timing his entrance for dramatic effect. The six-foot-two man whipped off his raincoat and made straight for Jack, a wide smile curling under his broad nose. "Guess you're surprised."

Hugh pulled out a chair, folded his red scarf on the side table, placed his gloves neatly on top, and draped the wet raincoat on the back of a sidearm.

"So, Hugh, how exactly did you know I stay at this hotel? What are you doing here? Not working on ships by the looks of you."

"No, gave up the sea years ago. I'm working with the government now, doing some work in the Middle East."

"So you're teaching ESL?"

"Making ends meet, Jack. Even have a little money to spend."

"Good. I could use some. When Iran blew up, it cost me a fortune and screwed up a great romance."

"Maybe there is something we could do together." Hugh's grin was accented by his spreading palms.

Jack folded his arms tight across his chest. His intuition told him this wasn't about their old sailing days. "What's up?"

A waiter ducked between them, placing a baker's basket of flaky croissants and warm scones on the table.

"Shokran," said Hugh, laying down a five-pound note.

"*Shokran* is Arabic, Hugh. The waiter is Persian, speaks Farsi. Say 'Merci.'"

Hugh's knowing smile caught Jack short.

"Correct," Hugh said.

Ah, so Hugh was testing. But for what?

"Renewing our old friendship is nice, but I came here because I need your help. There are very few people who could do the work we need," Hugh said. The noise in the room ebbed for a moment; he lowered his voice and continued. "Would you be interested in a job that could help us improve the relationship between the US and the UK?"

"No, I've got enough problems."

"We've watched you for months. My team knows the names of your friends in the Middle East, your clients, even your girlfriends. You speak Arabic with a classical Egyptian accent, and you're held in high regard by important people from the Sudan to Saudi Arabia."

"Who's we? The CIA?" Curiosity and anger swept through Jack's body in conflicting waves. He pushed his chair back from the table.

"Jack, we know you were in Iran when our embassy was overrun by those militant bastards. You were lucky to get out."

"Except that 80 percent of my business was in Iran, and 100 percent of my heart. My girlfriend is still stuck in Iran, taking care of her sick sister, but I'm going to find a way to get them out."

Hugh tapped Jack's knee and said, "What if I told you I could help you get them out?"

Jack sat very still, controlling his frustration. "Let me guess. You can only help me if I help you."

"Bingo! You help me, and I help you get your girlfriend. Simple as that."

The earnestness in Hugh's voice stirred Jack's deepest emotions. *Could some crazy US government plan get Farideh and Leah out of Iran?* Every angle he had tried led to a dead end. The last deal he made with two revolutionary guards cost him five grand and produced nothing. Jack looked around the room. Most diners had left. No one was close enough to eavesdrop on Hugh's low-toned whispers.

"First of all," Hugh said, "I can't use any of my guys, and the Brits want to stay out of it. I need someone outside the company to pick up the ball, kind of running an errand or two."

"The company?"

"Yeah, you know, the company—the CIA. My plan is a little complicated, but it will work because I have found the key."

"Nice going. CIA must be *so* proud of you," Jack said.

Ignoring Jack's sarcasm, Hugh continued. "The key to its success is to get a little assistance from someone who rolls through the world of international business with ease."

"Like me?"

"No, Jack, not *like* you. I *mean* you," Hugh said, finishing the last bit of his croissant and brushing golden flakes off his blazer. "I need your help with an arms dealer, a genuine scumbag. He provided the weapons those radical Islamic students used to take over our embassy.

"It'd be easy to get this guy out of the picture—neutralized. But we want more than that. We want all his contacts—his entire network. Which means we need his ledger. Washington and London will go through it, break down every one of his suppliers, find what country they're in and exactly who they are, where their kids go to school, and then"—he jabbed Jack's knee again, harder—"eradicate them from the planet." He clapped his palms together, making a sound like a gunshot.

Hugh leaned against the padded back of his chair, crossed his legs, and stared at Jack. "My plan went up the chain at MI6. The top brass want the creep's logbook too, but they can't do it themselves; they're restricted by bureaucrats in Parliament. When Langley approved my deal, MI6 came aboard."

Jack's mind raced, filtering spy-speak into a British breakfast with an old friend who was heaping confusion and mystery into his well-ordered life.

"I'll lay it all out for you; it's simple. You'll be able to carry out my plan as an undercover agent," Hugh said. "But, there is a complication. You would have to accept that the United States would not support you, or ever admit any knowledge of the plan, and would deny that you even exist. Same goes for MI6."

Jack's stomach clenched.

Hugh waited a moment, letting it all set in, then added, "This job will take balls, and you have them. I've seen you in action; you can do this."

"How long have you been watching me?"

"You're missing the point."

"How long?"

"We started watching you a year ago, before the embassy takeover in Tehran. Look, you came to the attention of the CIA because of your off-track business travels and your network of connections."

Jack was furious he had been spied on, astonished he had not noticed. He wondered how many people were spied upon by the government and knew he was not alone. "I'm pissed I didn't notice anyone was spying on me."

"No, you couldn't have guessed. We're very good at our work. You talked with two of our guys last week," Hugh said. "Remember the Carrier Air Conditioning vice president at the bar in the Damascus Sheraton?"

Jack's voice was barely a whisper. "Seriously?" He knew, to the core of his soul, that whatever he heard from Hugh would not even be close to the whole story. Hugh was a spy. Managing the truth is what spies do for a living.

Hugh carried on. "The USSR wants access to warmwater ports, so they're making deals and advising the Iranians how to handle the hostages to avoid an American rescue attempt. If those radical Muslim terrorists take over Iran, the country will be finished. The weapons supplier is the problem."

"How am I supposed to get close to the weapons supplier?"

"You know him."

"What do you mean I know him?"

"It's Mustafa Khaki."

Jack nodded while bells gonging in his brain were about to blow off the top of his head. If Hugh was looking for a shocked reaction, Jack would not let him have it.

"You spent a weekend with his daughter on the Caspian Sea. If Khaki found out, would he assume you were playing backgammon?"

Jack jumped up, threw his napkin at Hugh, and said, "I'm not betraying my girlfriend's father. I'm gone."

Hugh grabbed his coat, the long red woolen scarf flying around his neck. In the sweeping movement, it coiled into the collar of his trench coat. He followed Jack through the double doors, and they stepped off the carpeted steps and onto the icy sidewalk of Chesham Place.

"It wasn't backgammon?" Hugh's smile was evil.

Jack stuffed both hands into his overcoat pockets and walked west on the mansion-lined street. His mind raced back to the magical night with Farideh, the most beautiful, most intelligent, and most passionate woman he had ever met. The spark between them had grown, and then one night, lying in the grass on a hillock above the moonlit Caspian Sea, they had agreed their relationship would be exclusive; it would be built on love, on caring, on loyalty. They would support each other and care for each other, and their love would last forever. Their wedding would take place in Tehran around the time of the Nowruz holiday, when Tehran would be waking up from winter. They would never have guessed the Islamic Revolutionary Guard would overthrow the shah, tear the country apart, and make a Persian wedding impossible.

Traffic on the one-way street moved to the left. Jack turned right, pulling the lapels of his raincoat over his scarf. An elderly lady bundled in a stout raincoat stepped into the Diplomat Hotel as they passed. No one else was on the block.

"I've taken the liberty to arrange a preliminary meeting for you tomorrow with the head of MI6," said Hugh. "The chief and his associates will fill you in. Here's the address; take it." Hugh slipped the paper into Jack's coat pocket.

"Who said I was doing it?" Jack shot. "I'm not committing." They walked close, like English university schoolmates, heads bowed against the wind. Jack fingered the card in his pocket, wishing it was not there but curious enough to let it sit while he learned more. "Two spy agencies want me to give up my business and risk my life; and if anything were to go wrong, both would deny I exist? Why would I do such a stupid thing? And you can forget the 'your country needs you' stuff. You're out of your mind, Hugh. You'll have to tell your bosses you need to find someone else. I'm going back to the hotel." As he turned, his foot slipped on a wet leaf.

Hugh caught Jack's arm and spun him around. Nose-to-nose, eye-to-eye, and breath-to-breath, they stared at each other. "You're in, Jack. You are *in*," he said slowly, deliberately, enunciating each word as if his voice alone could carve words in stone. The speech was colder than the frigid air. "You're in because I can save your girlfriend just like I saved your skinny white ass in that hurricane. You're in even if you don't know it yet."

The storm tumbling in Jack's mind eased a bit when he looked into Hugh's eyes and saw calm in the eye of the hurricane and remembered the moment Hugh had caught him by the ankles when he got slammed by a giant wave and was heading over the side of the ship.

"Jack, hear this. That son of a bitch Khaki is not going to let his daughter leave Iran. He's lying to you if he says it'll happen. The only way you can get your girlfriend out of Iran is with my help." Hugh dropped his hands from Jack's shoulders, stood back, and waited.

Jack stepped to the left around Hugh and headed back to the hotel. Since childhood, curiosity had been one of Jack's motivating characteristics. Janice Joplin's tune ran through his mind: "Freedom's just another word for nothin' left to lose."

Jack looked back over his shoulder, cocked his head, and said, "I'll think about it."

When Jack's meeting at Coutts Bank in Mayfair ended, he decided to walk back to the hotel through Hyde Park. The jewelry store at Shepherds Bush corner still glittered with Christmas bunting, beckoning young lovers to buy a ring. The centerpiece in the window, a diamond crowning a silver band, would be perfect for his love, but he would wait and get a better deal in Kuwait. He walked onto the park's path lined with trembling young trees that had lost their leaves. Saplings wove like skeletons of a winter's famine but did not bow, holding out for spring. The park was quiet, the tourists gone. There were a few dogs walking their masters, some bike riders, and Jack. He valued the solitude of a long walk.

The knowledge that he was the target of a professional spy operation bore into his soul. Deep, conflicting emotions shadowed Jack through the park, around the serpentine, and across the guards' horse path toward Sloan Street. His emotions were churning with apprehension and a tumbler of fear. It was a two-sided conundrum: to save Farideh, he would need to betray their relationship by destroying her father. In his mind's eye, he saw his life draining away. His merchant banking business was threatened. His clients in Iran had gone underground, and his accounts were frozen in

Tehran's banks. But here was a chance to get Farideh back in his arms and out of Iran so they could build their life together and he could relocate his business.

The walk had become so mechanical that Jack was surprised when he arrived at the front door of his hotel. The solitary walk had become a funnel to a conclusion. He needed to learn more about Hugh, the CIA, MI6, and their plans. Tomorrow he would keep the appointment Hugh had made; he had the address:

> Century House
> 100 Westminster Bridge Road, WC1
> 10.00 a.m. 8 January 1980
> Office of the Chief

The cold night allowed only restless sleep and an early hot shower. Jack dressed quickly and pounded down the carpeted stairs to the lobby. "Starvin'," he said to the concierge, whose gleaming brass keys were getting a final rub before he fixed his emblem to his lapel. Harry had earned the honor of joining the select rank of tuxedo-dressed hotel impresarios after thirty years at Ladbroke's, providing service to the entitled, the snobs, the pretenders, and the cheaters, and then a second generation of snobs, pretenders, and cheaters. He kept a voluminous Rolodex of regulars, liked most of the guests, and especially liked Jack, who never failed to ask about his family or when he'd get a vacation or why he hadn't yet bought a ticket to come to America, where Jack promised to show him around.

Harry's usual broad smile was missing; so was the customary cheery welcome. "Aw' right, Mr. Devlin? Everything quite aw' right?"

"It is, Harry. And you're fine this morning?"

"Quite, sir, and I hope ya had a good meeting with yer friend at breakfast yesterday. Seemed a nice sort. Someone ya were in the army with?"

Harry had a way of eking out information by supplying a possible answer for whatever question he asked.

"Never been in the army, Harry. We met on a ship—a big iron ore carrier. Sailed together."

"Right, sir, of course. Nice man, though." Harry grinned. "Gave me a fiver when 'e left the note the day before yesterday and another when 'e left this one today."

"Today? Mr. Ebanks was here today?"

"'E was, sir, 'bout an hour ago. Said 'e had something of yers; put it in this envelope. Said ya'd understand. Nice man, fiver an' all that."

Jack knew his startled response was nectar for the concierge, who smirked and handed over the envelope. Walking toward a lobby chair, he noticed Harry watching him. Jack sat down, broke the seal, and pulled out a folded white note. It held a business card—his. The note was short.

> Jack,
>
> Believe this is your card. Nice of you to offer to help your seatmate, Jim Kendall, one of our top guys.
>
> I'll come by later to hear how your meeting went with the chief.
>
> H. E.

Jack flipped the card over and read, in his own handwriting:

> Ladbroke's Hotel, Belgravia
> 072 0267 4762

He rushed out through the lobby doors, sucked in the cold air, and leaned against the building. It had snowed lightly during the night, jamming traffic to a horn-honking, icy standstill on Pont Street. The noise was lost in the trance gripping his mind, which was spinning with more questions, more doubt, and more anxiety than he'd ever felt. He absently traced circles in the snow with his classic Church's Derby lace-ups. The cold air turned his breath into a close fog. He stepped back inside and headed for the concierge.

"Harry, need to make an international call; charge it to my room. Anyone in the booth?"

"No. Give Bridie the number. She plugs calls into Kuwait all the time."

"Not Kuwait."

"That's all right, sir, not Kuwait then. Bridie's your girl."

Before the end of his shift, Harry would know Jack had called Farideh.

Jack closed the door on the booth, picked up the phone, and gave the operator the number for Khaki's residence.

"On the line, Mr. Devlin. Scratchy though. Jiggle the dial if any trouble, sir."

"Thanks, Bridie."

"Farideh, it's Jack."

"Finally. Where are you?"

"London."

"It's getting worse here. The riding club is closing next month. Religious police are everywhere. Tehran is in chaos. I'm terrified every time I go out."

The scratchy connection did not hide the sound of Farideh crying.

"I know this is awful for you, honey, but I'm making good progress on a plan to get you out."

"My father is now as ballistic as his guns. I'm scared of him and his bodyguards."

"I know. It's going to take some time, but I promise I will get you out of Iran."

Farideh said, "I know you will. I love you."

And then silence.

Bridie came on, "Mr. Devlin, hate to tell you, but I was listening. Wasn't meself that lost the call. I think someone was listening in. They cut the line."

Jack knew that if anyone was listening in, it would have been Ali, her father's bodyguard.

"Okay, Harry, done with call. Here's an address I must get to. What's the best route?"

"That's Spy's Corner. You want to go to Spy House?"

"Right, I've heard it's a museum. Might be interesting, and I've got some time to kill."

"Take a taxi. Every driver in London knows exactly where it is. And never mind the petrol station at the bottom; it's all a cover." Harry's smirk was expected. "Going to a museum now, are you? Killing time—that's a new one."

Jack walked outside and hailed a cab, gave the driver the address, and leaned back in his seat. In the rush hour traffic, the cab could not keep up with fast walkers. He reflected on the past two days, and his memory wandered back to his childhood home near the end of the Lorica Road where there was never any traffic. As a kid he knew that someday that road could take him to exciting places with more buildings than trees, maybe to a town bursting with excitement that had ships and trains and planes. Maybe he would even get on a plane someday and go to a faraway place—to a really big city like New York, more than a hundred miles away. It would be amazing. His childhood had flowed with a stream of dreams.

He had been a runaway, a merchant seaman, the college party boy, and both a successful and an unsuccessful businessman. He had toyed with the idea of becoming a spy since his grandfather gave him a Dick Tracy watch on his tenth birthday. That seemed like a long time ago.

FOUR

Algernon Trivelpiece, Master Spy

A bit after nine in the morning, the cold was intense as Jack Devlin arrived at the most famous spy headquarters in the world. Raised letters on a brass plate read "Amalgamated Textiles," hammered onto a massive Oxford door, its fading ocher stain a camouflage for years of wear. Shaking the rain from his umbrella, Jack placed his gloved hand on the brass doorknob; its cold penetrated the glove and sharpened his anxiousness. The imposing door warped open a crack and then gave way, its heft pulling him through.

Today he was entering the secret sanctum of spies and dead heroes. This was MI6, where everyone acted under a provision to protect Her Majesty, Queen Elizabeth, and her government. Jack had learned what the CIA wanted; now he would find out what MI6 wanted. *Will anyone try to find out what I want?*

He shed his raincoat, draping it over his arm as he walked through a narrow warren of long, dark halls. Bland office doors with small nameplates of imaginary textile companies were separated by small windows whose damask curtains blocked the curious. The polished wooden stairs, which he took two at a time, creaked under his deliberate steps leading to the first floor. Under door number 101A, a plaque read "Office of the Chief." Before he could knock, the door opened. A short, dark-skinned man held it for a moment, rose to his tiptoes, peered over Jack's shoulder, and motioned him in. Jack recognized him as a Gurkha—a member of the force known for legendary Indian courage and valor in battle.

The Gurkha had the complexion of dark chocolate. His half shirt of soft reds and greens contrasted incapably with a gray highlands jacket and a silver rayon vest, accentuating shiny leggings billowing from a cummerbund to his upturned slippers.

"Gurkha brigade?" Jack asked.

Beneath a thin waxed mustache, the man smiled, pointed to an emblem on his shoulder that displayed two crossed Nepalese kukris, and said, "Yes, never appear in public without these."

The small anteroom was covered with dark blue velvet wallpaper that had captured years of stale pipe and cigarette odors that would never go away. In the chamber, heat rose from a row of knocking, hissing radiators that lined the wall. At an uncluttered desk, the receptionist looked up, smiling. *She seems kind but out of place*, Jack thought, *not like a spy*. Spies are supposed to look dour and impassive—not pretty, not cheerful. He had been seeing spies everywhere since he met with Hugh. He could find out more about MI6 if the lady would agree to meet for a drink, but he decided not to ask, for now.

"I'm expected," Jack announced. "Name is Devlin."

"Oh yes, indeed you are expected, Mr. Devlin. Kindly be seated. Won't be a moment." She covered an open file on her desk.

During his night of half-sleep, Jack had dreamed he would be thrown out of the building within minutes of arriving. Rejections for important jobs had been common since he left college. "Sorry, Jack, we can't use you. Maybe later. Maybe not. Thanks for coming by." Jack knew the weight of rejection and expected it.

The receptionist rose from her desk. "Evelyn is my name, Mr. Devlin," she said, offering her hand before heading for an inner door. Her white angora sweater was tucked into a wide black patent leather belt that blended with her pleated, charcoal-gray skirt. Her trim body was steady; she appeared to be a woman of confidence. "The chief will see you now," she announced, moving to open the unmarked door.

For much of his life, Jack had regularly gone through unmarked doors—some real, some imaginary—looking for a new deal, a different adventure, someone to love. This door looked as though it would not be the same as all the rest. Jack suspected that it would be unlike any other he had ever walked through.

The chief's office was like a university library, wood-paneled and lined with bookcases. Above a fireplace, framed photos of college-aged men covered the mantel. One photo showed a smiling young man with wavy black hair. The frame was draped in black crepe.

Overhead a fan fluttered in quiet mortification, acknowledging its inability to clear clouds of cigar smoke rising from a spittoon-size ashtray. Algernon Trivelpiece and Agatha Murphy, the director and the deputy director of MI6, sat stone-faced. They did not look clandestine. Spies were supposed to look like those in the framed pictures. But then Jack thought, *Perhaps spies would be better off if they did not look like the men in the pictures.*

Skipping customary English gallantry for a visitor, neither rose to greet him. The lady struggled a bit to stub out her cigar before offering Jack a thick hand. Brits measure weight in equivalents of a fourteen-pound stone. Agatha Murphy's scale would have come from a quarry. She was dressed without color, wearing a black calf-length skirt over black tights. A chunky strand of drooping gray faux pearls hung over her woven fisherman's sweater. Fate had given her five feet six inches of height, and years of smoking had given her a commanding baritone. She could have had Jack for lunch, dessert, or both.

"You look Irish. What are you?" asked Agatha.

"American, madam."

"Don't call me madam." Her words cracked like a whip.

"Yes, ma'am," said Jack with a bright smile.

In a calm tone, Trivelpiece said, "Thank you, Deputy Director."

Algernon Trivelpiece had the pall of a pallbearer but looked like the one to be borne. A setting with Trivelpiece as a professor reading *The Canterbury Tales* to schoolboys in knickers would have been more believable than Trivelpiece as the chief of MI6.

Hugh had told Jack that the deputy director, "Plentiful Agatha," had a low opinion of Americans, especially those in the intelligence service. However, Jack would find the chief was always a gentleman, always the spy master.

Agatha stood and walked across the room. She waddled like a fat lady dancing. Hugh had told him that in her younger days she could sneak up on a target, reach around, slit their throat, and be gone before the body dropped to the floor.

Agatha skipped formalities, getting right to the point. "You've met our target twice, we've learned. The fool's name is Khaki. We know this Khaki has a beautiful daughter and you've been taking advantage of her," she said.

"Is that what you women are calling it now? Taking advantage?" Jack said.

"Khaki is feeding the fires of the Iranian revolution, and we want to take away the fuel. He is the biggest arms merchant in the Middle East—maybe the world. You were brought in because of your relationship with his daughter. Name is Faniday or Famiday, something. Do you think your girlfriend is also involved in the arms trade?"

"Absolutely not, sir. Keep her out of this," Jack said. "And her name is Farideh. She would never be involved in this kind of business. She probably has no idea what her father does. She does not like him."

"You sure about that, Mr. Devlin?"

Jack bristled as Trivelpiece continued. "Her sister is sickly, a drain on Khaki's patience, and a constant interruption to his business deals. She is in need of medical supplies, which is where you come in, Mr. Devlin; it is your ticket back to Iran."

"How do you know about Farideh and Leah and her kidney disease?" Jack tucked his hands into his armpits, his elbows locked against his ribs. "Have you ever been to Iran?"

The old man flipped his palms up. "Go ahead, Deputy."

"No, but you have. Here is a photo of you in a park with some skinny bird. Farideh, maybe. Can't see your hands in the photo though. Busy, I guess."

"I love Farideh in that dress," Jack said.

Trivelpiece grinned and walked behind his deputy, placed his hands on her shoulders, and said, "You are a cool one, Mr. Devlin."

Discomfort and grave irritation roiled in the pit of Jack's stomach. Everyone—the CIA, Hugh, and the big shots of MI6—knew about his business, his lifestyle, his girlfriend, and even her family. The wounds to his privacy were no longer superficial. "The cool part of this deal is that we need each other," he said.

Plentiful Agatha continued. "Right, but your job is to stop that Persian slob, Khaki, by getting his list of sources and customers. After you do, kill him if you wish. If you get caught, a story will appear stating that you were Irish Republican Army trying to buy weapons." She smiled. "I'd kill you for that myself.

"We know that Farideh hates her father, but for some stupid reason she apparently likes you." Plentiful dropped her voice to a deeper rasp, letting the comment sink in. "I don't say that I agree with her choice in men, but ..."

She stopped midsentence. Her attention turned to a creaking oak door almost hidden between bookshelves at the opposite side of the room. Fully opened, it challenged any remaining collectedness Jack might have had. Hugh Ebanks stepped in past the shelves of tattered books, smiling broadly. "Hey, Jack. I was in the building. Thought I'd stop in to see how you're getting on."

Agatha sent a thick bubble-lipped air kiss and said, "Hugh, you said this guy would be an amateur, and you were right."

The chief straightened in his chair, grimacing. His expression reflected difficulties in trying to adjust the osteoporotic curve of his back. He rose, grasping a blackthorn walking stick with a well-worn knuckle at the top, to support his steps across the chamber to shake hands with Hugh. The chief's black greatcoat accentuated his hump. Trivelpiece's pithy expression was the kind found in the hospice ranks of the nearly departed.

A signal passed, Hugh nodded, and Trivelpiece turned to Jack. "Through an intermediary, we will get word to Khaki that a young American man, whom he knows, could help source and supply medicine for Leah's illness, and that he can be reached at Le Méridien Hotel in Kuwait."

Jack's scoffed. "So I'm the young man?"

"I'm sure Mr. Khaki will call to invite you to Iran, and I'm sure you'll find a way to get there."

The chief's voice had the timbre and command of a younger, stronger man. If superior intellect could be hidden behind a low profile, no one would be better at it than Algernon Trivelpiece.

Jack was about to carry out orders given to him in the clandestine office of a gargantuan pear-shaped woman and a man who needed only a top hat to look like a chimney sweep. They were the authors of what could become the biggest mistake of his life.

FIVE

Pandora Quince

The decision to accept the challenge thrown out by Hugh and Trivelpiece resulted in a daily training agenda that began the next morning.

The Gurkha sentry allowed a slight smile of recognition, standing as militarily stiff as one could in a satin uniform. The chocolate-skinned man nodded, ushering Jack in.

Evelyn rose from her desk, extending a soft white hand. "Good morning, Mr. Devlin, welcome back. Did your meeting with the chief go well yesterday?"

"It did, Miss Evelyn; it was very interesting."

Evelyn's cheerful greeting and the warmth of her handshake made Jack feel especially welcome.

She pushed her hair back, focused her intense blue eyes, and said, "Smart lady, the deputy director. Well respected around here. Mr. Trivelpiece is the boss, however; make no mistake. We do exactly as he says. What about your evening?"

"Dinner alone at the Enterprise on Walton Street. They have a lively bar and great food. Do you know the Enterprise? I think you'd like it."

Evelyn interrupted. "The Enterprise—that's where I met my husband. You'll find some lovely lasses there, Mr. Devlin."

Jack managed a muffled reply that he had been chatted up by a couple lovelies last night, which they both knew was a white lie. For now, he had an appointment with an MI6 guy—an instructor. "I was told to check in with you and ask for the Mountbatten Room."

"Of course, Mr. Devlin, you are meeting Agent Chapman. I'll let his department know you are here. Please sit down. He will come to fetch you."

As quickly as if he had been waiting around the corner, a well-dressed young man with broad shoulders and blond hair nodded to Evelyn and then said, "Mr. Devlin, I'm Chapman. This way, sir. Take your coat." Chapman had six inches on Jack. His crushing handshake engulfed Jack's hand. Chapman's formidable athletic body would have been welcomed by a rugby coach, and surely by the lasses at the Enterprise.

Jack stammered an all-American "See ya" to Evelyn, waved at the Gurkha, and followed Chapman down a hallway of echoes, lined with head-and-shoulder busts of nameless old spies.

"Going well, Mr. Devlin?"

"I had a nice talk with the receptionist, Evelyn. She is quite charming. Don't you think?"

Chapman frowned. "Yes, a sad story there. Her husband was killed last year in Istanbul. You might have seen his photo on the mantel in the chief's office—the one draped in black."

They entered a stadium-like room that needed only a couple of hoops to be a basketball court. It had half-paneled walls, a parquet floor, and three small windows near the ceiling. At the far end there stood a four-foot-high butcher-block table long enough for a six-footer to lie on. *But for what? Maybe a massage? No, maybe an autopsy.* He squelched a shudder. Long cabinets without handles lined the walls. In the center, under a caged lightbulb, Jack saw the high back of an old wooden wheelchair. There was not another stick of furniture in the room. Fascinated, Jack watched dainty white hands grasp the wheels to turn the chair toward him.

"Mr. Devlin, I presume."

The chair's occupant was one of the most stunning women he had ever seen. He tried to retract a dumb wave, mumbling, "Hi, my name is Jack. I'm new. American."

"I know who you are, sir," she said without a hint of welcome. "You are staring at my legs."

Tough lady, Jack thought. He could work with her. "What happened?"

"It was in Vienna, last year; an Egyptian. I made sure he did not get a second shot." A wry smile curled her lips. "I'm Pandora Quince, section chief, Middle East. Mr. Ebanks has spoken highly of you. In fact, he spoke very highly of you. Are you two in a relationship?"

The abrasive question knocked him off balance. "How can you ask such a ridiculous question? Of course not."

"A question, Mr. Devlin. Do you always react like that to unexpected questions? Did it throw you off?"

Jack's Irish blood boiled, fired by a thin girl in a wheelchair at least five years his junior. He had expected a polite, stuffy British interviewer, or some hardened master spy with whom he would talk, man-to-man, across a desk. Her question threw him off. It was his turn.

"Tell me, Mrs. Quince, how do you have sex?"

An exclamation exploded from the wheelchair. "Ha!" A strand of small white pearls bounced on her red wool sweater. "It's Miss. How do I have sex? With spectacular talent."

Jack caught a glimpse of the military shine on her unscuffed high-heeled black shoes poking out beneath a highland lap blanket. Pandora's petite hands held firm to the chair's wheels. She maneuvered it regally as if it were an extension of her body, riveting Jack's attention.

"To set things straight, Mr. Devlin, I'm responsible for keeping our brave men and women ready to defend themselves and meet the objectives of their missions, whatever and wherever they may be. You, a civilian sent to us by the CIA, are untrained. Agatha said you were the most untrained civilian we've ever seen. No idea where you'll fit in. Hugh Ebanks said you won't be working as a CIA agent; you're doing a favor for him—a single mission. You'll be a one-off. If you don't survive it, it won't be our problem."

Jack let the insult ride across the floor with Pandora's wheelchair as she rolled toward him.

"I am charged with arranging your training. I'll keep it very basic for your sake. We will see how sharp you are, how quickly you get through our process. Mr. Ebanks said you'd master it in a few days. Let's see."

She wheeled to a corner and pressed a brass button, opening a door. Two men stepped into the room and took places on either side of Chapman. They were dressed alike— generic university boys, Eaton maybe. "These men will become your best friends over the next few weeks. They will begin their assignments with you this morning. They are specialists in communications, weaponry, personal defense, and clandestine methods, and they are experts on the Middle East. You'll get along well."

"Won't take that long; I know the objective, and it'll get done."

When she spun away, Jack thought he caught a faint smile—a glint in her eye. In seconds she was gone.

Chapman spoke first. "Our task, Mr. Devlin, is to instruct you in the basics. You are not expected to be in real danger." Chapman had the bearing of a ranked officer and spoke with authority. "We're here to train you for a special mission. It should be quite simple. Follow us to the weapons room. Let's see how you hold a gun."

SIX

Fish, Chips, and Spy Craft

From dawn to dusk, Jack was led through the basics of covert operations by men who shared experiences that would never be known publicly. Jack learned how MI6 deciphered code, extracted confidences, and recognized enemy agents no matter how they dressed or acted, or to whom they had sworn allegiance. He felt accomplished when he took down his instructor. That elation dissipated when the guy snuck up behind him and put him in a headlock while he was bragging to Chapman.

On a crisp March morning, Jack received a pat on the back and instructions from Chapman. "Report to the lady in the wheelchair."

At an office marked "Section Chief M. E.," he knocked once, opened the door, and found Pandora in her wheelchair, head down, focused on a file.

Agent Chapman had said Pandora Quince was only the second woman to hold the job after Plentiful Agatha was promoted to deputy director in 1978. Both women understood the depth of the MI6 culture—its role in government and in polite society. They had learned it was okay to cheat, steal, lie, and deceive everyone except their partners. It was unisex; women fought just like men. After all, a spy is a spy.

Pandora looked up and slid her wheelchair back. "Neglected to bring lunch today. Have you eaten, Mr. Devlin?"

"Not yet, Miss Quince."

"Stick with Pandora, please. I fancy fish and chips; there's a shop in the high street." Pandora brought her thin hands together, slipped on black leather gloves, and grasped both wheels. Her long brown hair, secured in a ponytail, bobbed when she adjusted her hips on the paisley seat cushion. A blue sweater hid all but a crisp white collar, scalloped at the neck. If she could have stood, her ivory wool skirt would have touched the floor. Jack was again surprised to see her high-heeled shoes. Sneakers—"trainers," as the Brits called them—would have been expected. *But why not?* he thought. *Maybe she wears them with a dream to dance again, take a stroll on the strand, walk to the top of Leith's Hill … someday.*

Pandora took Jack to an elevator down to the car park and the alley behind MI6. Crunching through crusted snow, Jack walked next to the wheelchair and kept up a stream of conversation. "Shame these sidewalks don't get plowed," he said.

"No need; this old wheelchair has a powerful engine."

"Right. You move it with ease. Almost like you have years of experience."

The line at Rock & Sole Plaice parted for Pandora's chair which she moved forward deliberately. Jack followed, tossing thank-yous to the disturbed crowd in the line. At a table for two, he stepped ahead of Pandora, removing a chair. He draped her plaid blanket over the chair's handles and grabbed a couple menus off the bar, keeping the soggy one.

"Don't really need a menu, Mr. Devlin, just fish, chips, tea later. Now, let's get back to you. What have you learned over the last several weeks?"

"If I were headed into a deadly mission, I'd want Chapman by my side. He gets Spy Craft 101."

Banging plates, giggling office girls, and street clatter from the partially open door ensured their conversation would be as safe as if in her office. Pandora chuckled, acknowledging Jack's jibe.

"The lads said you're as cautious as you are reckless. You take chances after quick analysis. You've a flavor for cultures and language, and you find a way to fit in wherever you go. They said you can tell where someone is from after they've spoken just a few words."

"Maybe."

"And you can carry on basic conversation in seven or eight languages."

"Maybe."

"And you correctly identified where nine people came from by how they dressed."

"But there were ten pictures. I missed one. What does that tell you, Miss Quince?"

"Call me Pandora, please, unless we're in the office. And it tells me that you're too much your own man to be accepted into MI6."

Jack felt attacked by a handicapped woman against whom he had little defense. He played an imaginary game of chess using the salt and pepper, with malt vinegar as the queen, until a waiter interrupted, plopping down two baskets of crisp battered plaice on a bed of greasy chips.

"Don't worry; you're not applying for a long-term job with our service. Hugh asked us to train you because the CIA could not."

Pandora did not have any passion for collaboration with the CIA except when Hugh's name came up.

"We have strong feelings here for Mr. Ebanks," she said. "He tracked two KGB operatives from an apartment in the area of Parliament to a flat off Derby Gate and dispatched them both—saving the lives of hundreds had their bombs gone off. We're in his debt. If not for him, you would not be sitting here with me eating fish and chips.

"Mr. Trivelpiece is waiting to have a final talk with you." Pandora placed her rumpled napkin on the plate, clicked the wheel brake off, and backed away from the table. She stopped for a moment and said, "Our training makes you a better man. Maybe not our kind of man, but that's okay; the training was free."

Jack chuckled, picked up the check, and said, "Apparently you wanted to have lunch in case you never see me again."

"You might be right."

Blustering winds separated afternoon clouds over London after dusting it with snow. The chill lost some of its grip when the winter sun found gaps among the clouds, blessing those who raised their faces against the wind to catch a few rays. The remainder of their lunch talk had been about "the business," except for a few diversions that crept into comments about faraway places like minarets in Cairo and the fierce winds from the deserts of Iran. Pandora had learned more about him than he liked, but not everything.

Jack bent hard against the cold afternoon wind, watching Pandora's heavily gloved hands push the spoked wheels through the wet snow. She ignored his offers to help, climbing curbs in full command of her vehicle, if not her legs. Jack had to jog the few blocks to keep up with the speedy section chief, sloshing narrow tracks on the sidewalk. Irritated, he said in a loud voice, "Hey, slow down a bit. What's the big rush?"

Pandora moved faster, not stopping until she reached the stairs to the office. "Steps are not for me. I'll go back around to the car park elevators. Go ahead up; Agent Chapman will be waiting for you. Thanks for lunch." Swiveling, she turned toward the alley between the gray stone buildings. Jack waited and watched her turn right, almost disappear, and then wheel back. "Anything wrong?" she asked, sounding cross.

"No, nothing. I'm going up now," said Jack, feeling like a schoolboy caught skipping afternoon class.

Agent Chapman stood at the top of the granite stairs. "Afternoon, Mr. Devlin. Everything all right? Nice lunch?" He displayed the impatience of an Etonian upper classman jousting with a "new boy."

"Hope you didn't say I was too harsh with your training."

"Sorry, agent, your name never came up," Jack said, climbing the stairs two at a time. He shrugged snowflakes off his shoulders and handed his coat to Chapman. He looked for a reaction, but Chapman was deferential. In the clandestine world, deference lessened caring, protecting feelings. *Another time, another place*, Jack thought, *I could have been friends with Chapman.*

"I've been told to take you up to the chief's office."

Jack made eye contact, playfully wagging his finger to admonish Chapman. "The chief is referred to only as C, Agent Chapman; apparently you forgot."

Chapman turned at the door to Evelyn's office and said, "Good luck, Mr. Devlin; nice to have met you. Have a nice life." He shut the door harder than necessary, bringing a wry smile to Evelyn's face.

SEVEN

There Will Be Chaos

Jack had worked hard and felt prepared to handle whatever would happen in C's office. He had been taught by every instructor that he needed to appear unchanged. No one was ever to suspect that he had become a spy, no matter how improbable. His excitement would have to remain stuffed once he walked out onto London's busy streets.

"Come in, Mr. Devlin; good to see you again." Algernon Trivelpiece rose, bending his long frame to shake hands, tossing Evelyn a smiling nod that meant she was dismissed. C's manner was friendly and deliberate. He clapped Jack on the shoulder, steering him to a burgundy leather chair. On a side table sat a box of matches, a copy of *Punch* magazine, an ashtray, and a bottle of scotch. C grabbed the bottle by the neck, poured a glass, and continued. "Join me in a whisky? I can tell you like scotch."

How nice, Jack thought. *A belt with the boss.* "Yes, I will, thank you. I recognize that scotch—Chequers, single malt." Jack came off like an old friend but wished he hadn't.

"You apparently like whisky, Jack. I've heard you like gin too ... and beer?"

"Yeah, beer too. It's wine I don't like—time waster."

Trivelpiece paused, the twinkle in his eye keeping Jack on the edge of his seat. Pouring the rich amber scotch, Trivelpiece said, "We're hard drinkers in this business, Mr. Devlin, but we must know how to drink and when—and especially with whom." Jack knew any background check would have identified his occasionally notorious drinking habits. Trivelpiece filled Jack's glass halfway, raised his own, and said, "A toast to you, sir. Completed our training program marvelously, I'm told. Brilliant."

Jack avoided rolling his eyes, thinking, *Only the Brits would use the word "brilliant" to describe an action.* He wondered how they described diamonds.

"Terrible situation in Iran, Mr. Devlin. Sorry about your countrymen being held by those devils."

"I was in Tehran that day, Chief."

"It must have been hard for you."

"I was stuck in a smelly bedroom for days, listening to gunshots, hoping the embassy staff had been released and that we'd get back to normal. Then I found there was no going back. I had enough money to bribe my way onto a flight to Kabul, then flew to Kuwait."

Trivelpiece nodded and changed the subject, lowering his voice. "Russia was intimately involved in that takeover. They were working with Ayatollah Khomeini from his exile in Marseille. Yevgeny Primakovski was directing the operation from a KGB office in Moscow. We know him well, but the CIA never knew that he and Khaki were working together."

Khaki's involvement with the Revolutionary Guard did not surprise him, but Russian involvement? He began to formulate a sentence about Khaki's mother until he realized that would be Farideh's grandmother. "Farideh's father is a son of a bitch."

"That he is, Jack, and so is Primakovski. But there is a way to stop the Russians from gaining more influence. The Americans are looking for a soft underbelly in Primakovski's Middle East section. Given your knowledge of Arabic and the Middle East, as well as your contacts, you can venture where an Englishman cannot. We may also require your involvement with a man called the Translator—a KGB officer who has just made contact with the West."

Jack's heart skipped two beats. "KGB? Insane. The game is changing."

Trivelpiece shrugged. "We'll talk about this with Ebanks, son; it is not our idea, so let's continue talking about Iran. If the Americans attempt to rescue the hostages, and no doubt they will try, Tehran will be in chaos. The only chance to neutralize Khaki and extract your ladies is to do it now. You'll have three weeks—four at the most."

EIGHT

The oak door between the bookshelves opened. Pandora Quince rolled her old wooden wheelchair into the room, tossing a cheery "Good afternoon."

She picked up on Trivelpiece's comments directly. "When Khomeini was exiled by the shah, he went to Iraq and met a general called Saddam Hussein. On the second day of their meeting, a Persian arms dealer showed up."

"I'll guess. Mustafa Khaki."

"Right. They made arrangements for truckloads of guns and ammunition to be shipped out of Saddam's stockpile to Khomeini's followers. The guns that were used to capture your countrymen came from that lot."

Jack wrung his hands in cold desperation. The father of the most beautiful girl in Iran was a monster. Jack shook his head and stared at Pandora and the chief as gusts of snow rattled the windowpanes. Nothing rattled Pandora or the chief.

Pandora leaned forward. "He's got to be taken out. Our assets in Iran are frozen. Guns are flying into the hands of radicalized teenagers. Khaki's machine needs to be dismantled."

"Neutralize my girlfriend's father? Romantic."

She moved her wheelchair farther from the drafty windows, which gave Jack a different angle to see through the herringbone footrests. The inclined high heels presented a puzzling picture. The shoes were scuffed.

Pandora caught his stare and turned her wheelchair. "I'm only concerned about the mission—not luck, not hurricanes ... not if we've gotten this far." She straightened her lap blanket and flared it to cover her feet. The woolen reds and greens flowed simply, bleeding into one another.

The chief watched Pandora adjust herself and then turned his attention to Jack and resumed. "In our business, things may not be quite as they seem. Cover stories are created, based on contrivances. Generally, people choose to believe, not to question. Those that are extremely bright may see through a story but will never let you know. Those are the smart ones. Those are the kinds of people we want in our service."

Jack felt he was the object of the chief's speech.

"It takes time and skill to set up cover stories, but you already have one." Clasping his age-scarred hands, the chief looked Jack directly in the eye. "The essence of good agents is that they are ordinary, accomplishing tasks like everyone else. But an agent must not allow slips, must master situations, and must never lose sight of the mission. Be ever aware, Mr. Devlin, that in spite of evident contradiction, we thrive on trust. An experienced agent gives up nothing but always gains the adversary's trust—unless, of course, it is the end of the game. When the final shot is fired, when falling to the floor dying, his last thought will be 'I shouldn't have trusted him.'"

"MI6 has been effective because of selection criteria—which you have now met, Mr. Devlin," said Pandora. "Your scores in cryptology and language exceeded our expectations. You have passed tests you knew about and a few you did not. Congratulations."

Trivelpiece stepped in front of the wheelchair to shake Jack's hand. Pandora punched a thin thumbs-up and reached down to lock her wheels.

Jack shook the chief's hand. He had been accepted. The weeks of rigorous training and tests were all over now. The realization that he had enjoyed the training was unforeseen.

"Oversight is ongoing. You'll never know it, but you'll be watched; you'll be monitored. That also means you will not be alone most of the time. The chief and I are convinced that when you are alone, you'll be okay."

"Robbing arms merchants' business plans for fun." His lips tightened. "Ha."

Trivelpiece ignored the comment. "You'll be paid in cash. All agents are paid cash. Saves bookkeeping, you know. Treasury lads have a certain code for our business—not subject to tax remittances." He grinned, handing over a thick envelope. "This is your up-front. There is enough in the packet to cover all expenses. Get rid of your personal credit cards; there is one in the envelope. But use cash to pay for planes and hotels. We run the kind of business here where record-keeping does not fit."

Jack took the envelope, thumbed its thickness, and slid it into his jacket pocket.

Stretching to pull a paper from a brown folder in the bottom of his desk, Trivelpiece's cadaver-like body creaked as he unsealed a wax-stamped folder and cleared his throat. "We have new information from Pandora's Iran desk." Trivelpiece paused at the second page for a moment. "The report says that Leonid Brezhnev, Russia's prime minister, met with Khaki and the Romanian president, Ceaușescu, in Bucharest twice to plan for the involvement of the Communist Party in Iran. Arming young rebels to start the revolution was done not only in the name of Islam; it was to tie Russia closer to the imams who will take over every village in the country. These extremist radicals have co-opted the top people in the Revolutionary Guard. The Iranian people still don't know how deeply the Russians are involved. By the time they do, it will be too late. They will have lost their country."

"I have spent a lot of time in Iran, love the people and the country. What has happened with the Revolutionary Guard and the radical students is devastating," said Jack.

"Agreed. And the taking of the hostages has now become a problem for Iran and"—he smiled—"for Russia. Our intelligence says that if the US wants to make a rescue attempt, they must do it quickly, while the hostages are still together. The Russians want Iran to spread them out until negotiations begin, when they can be useful pawns."

"Khaki is everywhere."

"He is indeed," Trivelpiece said, folding back into his chair. His habit of placing both gnarled hands on his knees before speaking was preceded by a long silence. "Everything depends on your successful completion of the mission."

"You'll be leaving tomorrow," Pandora said.

"To sum up, Mr. Devlin, the work you have done here over the last several weeks is commendable. You have the unqualified recommendation of Mr. Ebanks, along with the endorsement of the head of our Middle East Division." His eyes twinkled like a grandfather's when he looked at Pandora.

"You will find that Miss Quince has prepared explicit details. Commit the key points to memory; then destroy the file."

Pandora spoke authoritatively. "I endorsed you, Mr. Devlin, because you know the Middle East. You don't arouse suspicion. Apparently you have been 'going it alone,' as they say, for most of your life. Good. This is lonely work, and clearly you want the job."

Trivelpiece raised a long, thin piano finger to interrupt the discussion and rang the silver bell. The Gurkha appeared with a spritzer of soda and three glasses on a brass tray. He bowed slightly, placed the tray on the table, and then backed out of the room.

"Questions for Miss Quince?" said Trivelpiece while pouring drinks.

"Yes, I want to know why it was necessary to test me with tricks. I caught them all."

Clasping her hands, Pandora said, "I believe you did, Jack. Agent Chapman was unable to intimidate you. When he gave you meaningless tasks that tested your response to orders, you carried them out and then asked questions. You never jumped to conclusions."

Trivelpiece and Pandora sipped their drinks. Jack slammed his and hoped the chief would pour another. Instead the chief kept talking.

"Agent Devlin, there's another matter Pandora and I wish to counsel you about."

He had been called "agent" for the first time. He felt flushed but hoped it didn't show.

Trivelpiece crossed to the windows and drew the drapes open. Winter's dusk was descending on rooftops where gusts swept snow into the lee of knee-high roof walls, turning cracking icicles into wind chimes. The cold seeped into the chief's office, but even that did not trigger the offer of another scotch. "Pandora and I told you that gut instinct is of critical value in our work—and so is discretion, you understand. Let us ask a question or two."

"If you thought someone in MI6 might be a double agent, would you immediately report that to someone?" asked Pandora, continuing without waiting for an answer. "I ask because you solved our puzzles and remained discreet. You didn't speak out." Pandora's wheelchair slid to Jack's right. The blanket that warmed her lap began to move. It rustled as if she were crossing her ankles.

"We're waiting," stated Trivelpiece, glancing at Pandora.

"Well, Chief, I'd get into the matter, arrange a ploy, get my suspicion confirmed, then take action when I had confirmed it."

"Why not take action when you first suspected the subject might work for the other side?"

"I would neither act on suspicion nor ignore it. I might not report it even when convinced. There could be more to discover. Creating suspicion before confirmation would not be effective. I'd take my chances until instinct paired with fact. Until wheelchairs become jokes."

Pandora grasped the blanket, pulled it onto her lap, folded it neatly, and crossed her legs. "We knew you had discovered the wheelchair was a ruse but expected you would take action. You did not. You did not report your suspicions to the chief or to Agent Chapman. All the other candidates questioned the game and reported the wheelchair ruse as if they had discovered the Holy Grail. They were overwhelmed with their brilliance. None of them are still with us."

Glasses were raised. "To the queen, to the president." Pleasantries meant it was over.

Pandora rose from her wheelchair, placing her hand on Jack's arm.

"I'll walk you to the door, Agent Devlin. Meet me at Lulu's Club tonight. I've been saving a dance for you."

NINE

Furlong in the Belfry

Jack thudded into a black cab, clutching the envelope. He toyed with the idea of opening it but then caught a glimpse of the driver looking in his rearview mirror. He chuckled under his breath realizing he had to stop seeing a spy behind every steering wheel or hiding in every Hyde Park bush. MI6 and MI5 were made up of ordinary people: some full-time agency staff, some part-timers, retired policemen, schoolteachers, and maybe a bookseller or two among a corps of high-performing agents. Sherlock Holmes would not have been accepted in the game, one of his instructors had said, but his partner, Dr. Watson, had the right makeup. Jack would wait for the privacy of his hotel room to open the envelope.

Ladbroke's doorman pulled the glass door open from the inside, too smart to stand out in the cold. "Right, Mr. Devlin, you must see 'arry before you go up, sir, 'e's in a dither, 'e is. Everything all right?" The inquiring grin underlined the doorman's love for gossip.

"Everything is fine. I'll see Harry."

"Righty ho, sir."

Jack spotted the concierge through knotted crowds in the lobby; he was finishing up with four tourists.

"Yer dinner reservations at Mimmo d'Ischia 'r' confirmed. Seven o'clock. Doorman will see to a taxi." Harry waved them off and stepped away from the concierge desk.

"Come along, Mr. Devlin," he said without expression. Harry pushed the cloakroom door aside, waving Jack in. "Yer black friend was 'ere—rough-looking, shorty character with him. Cool customer 'at one. 'E knew ya belonged to Moismann's club. Gave me ten quid to book yer table. Said to tell ya to come right away."

The excitable concierge had worked hard to lose his protruding tummy and Cockney accent while projecting an upper-crust manner. He had not succeeded in either case. "'At fat little bloke was a foot taller 'n a dwarf. 'Owed 'e know yer favorite table is in the belfry at Moismann's? Mr. Devlin, sir, yer up to yer knickers. I'll send the big Paki porter along. 'E's one o' dem black ones; 'e can look out fer ya."

Jack placed his hands on Harry's gold epaulettes, glanced around as if anyone else could fit in the tiny space, and said, "You and I have known each other for so long we almost have a father/son relationship. My dad's gone, you don't have a son, so we look out for each other. I'm grateful."

"Aye, Jack, you've been nicer to me than any o' the lot come in 'ere. Yer all right, Jack. I hope ya won't change." Harry's grim look of concern had not eased.

Jack took his hands off Harry's shoulders, moderating his voice. "The black man, Mr. Ebanks, is an old friend—not a black friend, Harry, an old friend, like you. We're working together now, so don't worry. I'm off to Kuwait tomorrow, back here in a few weeks. I'll contact you if a problem comes up."

Harry looked relieved until Jack said, "On the remote chance of trouble, I'll send you a message to relay to a different friend." Jack took out his business card and wrote Pandora Quince's name and phone number on the back. "Harry, you're a good man. Thank you for being concerned. I'm going up to my room, getting a scarf, and putting something in my safe; then I'll walk over to Moismann's. Everything will be all right; no need to worry," Jack lied.

He left the concierge in a hurry, realizing he had changed. The not-a-care-in-the-world days were all gone, no longer free and easy. He was off to dinner in Moismann's Belfry with an old friend from the Cayman Islands and a tall dwarf.

Moismann's had once been an Anglican church. When the candles went out for the last time, a clutch of Orthodox Jewish real estate speculators bought the small church, converting it to a club with enough paying customers to make the rabbis smile. The coveted private table in the belfry was always held for the best customers—the biggest tippers. The maître d' dressed like a tuxedo ad and, by his own admission, was one of the best in London. He knew Jack well, greeting him with a slight bow. "No tip necessary, Mr. Devlin; your friends took care of it. They are waiting. Come through please."

They walked into the less-than-holy bar, passed the side altar, and went through the sacristy and up the narrow, red-carpeted stairs.

"Thanks, Andrew. Send the waiter up, please, with a bottle of Chequers, single malt."

"Oui, monsieur." His French accent was right out of East London.

Hugh stood, offered his hand, and said, "Congratulations, Jack. You're now officially an agent—sadly not one of ours. Let me introduce you to Eddie Furlong. MI6 is secretly proud of this man. He was chief agent-in-residence in Tehran."

"Hello, Jackie. I've heard about you. Nice background you got, laddie—almost believable."

Furlong looked like the kind of guy who would cross the street to walk in the shadows and avoid the light. "My background is what it is, Midge, and don't call me Jackie. What's this about?"

Hugh flipped the cover of an elegant leather box with the crest of the Cuban cigar maker José Martí and plucked a Cohiba. Furlong folded his ham fingers around a bulging Montecristo No. 4. Jack drew a Camel cigarette from his pack and used his Zippo to light up all three.

"Eddie has been teaching Middle East spy craft to agents from America, the UK, and Canada who work in the Middle East. He's trained the locals too and knows all of them."

"I'm now at the Middle East Center for Arabic Studies, near Beirut; speak Arabic and Farsi. I heard about you there."

"Ridiculous," Jack responded.

Furlong wagged his cigar at Jack. "No it ain't, kid. I know all about what happened when Bader Al-Quabendi and his brother screwed you on a deal in Kuwait. Both ended up in a hospital."

Jack waved his middle finger. "They must have slipped on banana peels."

Hugh held up his hand. "Lordy, Jack, Tehran is in chaos; getting some up-to-date background from Furlong could be the difference between life and death. He's trained half the spies in Iran and someday will probably save your ass. Cut him some slack."

Hugh elbowed Furlong, shoved the silverware aside, and glared at Jack. "I selected you for this mission, Jack; you gotta prove I made the right choice. Pandora complimented your success; now our reputations are on the line. Listen to this guy." Veins bulging on Hugh's temples said it was time to get serious.

"What did Trivelpiece tell you they expected other than Khaki's dismembered head and his files on a tray?" asked the shortest Furlong in London.

"Makes no difference what happens to Khaki, and it clearly makes no difference what happens to me," Jack said.

Furlong exhaled a cloud of cigar smoke and blustered, "We all know that son of a bitch, but we can't get to him." His pudgy face reddened. "Hugh told us you can because you know his daughter, so use her. Get him alone, then kill him. Do what you want with the girls."

Jack recoiled, boiling, his face scarlet. He had almost forgotten an instructor saying an assignment would be finalized in a "set" meeting. This was it.

Jack sat on the edge of his seat, turned away from Furlong, and bore in on Hugh. "You knew what my personal mission was—and still is. Get Farideh out of Iran, help her sister, Leah, and recover my money."

Hugh turned on his "so what" smile. "Come on; no way you can do either one without us. We gotta work together, all of us: you and me, this guy here, people you don't know but who know you and who know why you're to be protected."

Eddie started to interrupt.

"Shut up, Eddie; I'm talking. Jack's an old friend, and I'm taking care of him. Jack, as I told you, the ledger is worth a couple million bucks at least. The Israelis said they'd pay three million, but we can't let them or anyone else get it. That information belongs to the US, and I need to get my hands on it. I'm depending on you, my brother; do this for me." Hugh's voice had dropped to an altar boy's whisper.

Furlong argued, "Right, but MI6 gets to see it first."

"Don't screw with me, Eddie; this is our game, and Jack is our guy. MI6 will get a copy.

"Trust me, Jack; this is about Khaki and the ledger. You do what we want, guaranteed you get what you want. Your girls will be shopping in Paris in a couple weeks. We got you covered, including everything you lost when those goons burned down the bank in Karaj. You gotta trust me."

Hugh stood and buttoned his blazer. "Okay, let's wind this up," he said, taking Jack's arm. "Furlong's all right, Jack. He makes more noise than he should, but he knows what he's doing, and he will be tracking you. He and Pandora worked out the details.

"Jack, when you were last at Khaki's house, he told you he'd spare no expense to get the medication his daughter needs. Khaki doesn't want to waste time with Leah, but he can't kill her either. He wants her out of his hair and now believes he can't do that without your help. That's our leverage. That's how we get this mission done. Through your merchant banking connections, you can get the stuff he needs in a way that protects Khaki from drawing the attention of the Islamist rebels. He will need to see you in

Tehran, face-to-face. If anyone can sneak you in and out of Iran, it's Mustafa Khaki. It'll go like clockwork.

"When this is over, I want to meet this girl who has captured your heart. I'll buy dinner when you get her to Paris. Good luck, Jack."

TEN

Le Méridien, Kuwait

"**W**elcome back to Kuwait, Mr. Jack," said Le Méridien's doorman. The ending notes of a muezzin's sonorous chant blasted by loudspeakers signaled evening prayer—the one to comfort all during the night.

The white-robed Sudanese night bellman, Sabah, was shooing the important and the not-so-important out of "his" hotel. "No more rooms; fully booked!" Sabah shouted, whirling his broom like a Sufi dervish, eyes rolling, mind in a trance, sweeping the shiny marble lobby clean of infidels and a half-dozen or so noninfidels. He swept without prejudice; religion did not matter to him. "Out, out! *Ma-a salama*, no more rooms! *Yallah, yallah*, let's go!" Anyone who underestimated Sabah's focus learned quickly, catching the force of the reeds on a stick. Within minutes, Sabah's flailing broom moved the last straggler into the fog of humidity that covered Kuwait like a damp sponge.

Sabah spotted Jack and waved his broom in a welcoming swish, his resplendent white robes flowing with each swing. "*Allah* be praised; you are back, Mr. Jack. *Tamam, tamam*, it is good."

"I went to London to close a deal, Sabah."

"If it is not the truth, Mr. Jack, I have some truth for you." Sabah grinned, his coal-black eyes gleaming. "Your room has been held, and"—another too-long-pause—"you have an important message."

Sabah was a Dinka—a southerner from Juba in the south of the Sudan. His black skin, white robes, and the white turban wrapped around his head gave him an imposing presence, like that of a paraclete from the desert. Behind his smile, perfectly white teeth gleamed in a tribal-scarred, perfectly black face. Sabah didn't smile often, reserving it for special friends like Jack.

"Truth, Mr. Jack, is that people believe you are a good friend. True, isn't it? You would do anything for your friends, even Sudanese ones." He winked. "Even Persian ones?"

The question surprised Jack.

Beckoning him to follow, Sabah shuffled toward the bellman's desk—the central office of his thriving nightly enterprise. Jack guessed Sabah had pocketed hundreds of dinar from men who needed a room. He always held a few open to keep his reputation and his cash flow positive.

Sabah lowered his voice, "A man has telephoned for two days; calls himself Ali." Sabah's bloodshot eyes swiveled quizzically to see who lurked nearby. "He wishes you call, day or night."

Jack read the slip of paper Sabah had extracted from a hidden pocket in the folds of his robe.

> Office of M. Khaki
> 98 021 921 9688
> Tehran

"Man say Mr. Khaki your friend?"

"My friend is Mr. Khaki's daughter, Farideh."

Sabah stood tall, staring at Jack. "By the grace of Allah, I pray you are not going to try to get into Iran. Americans put in jail, killed every day."

Jack shook his head and crossed his fingers behind his back. "No, Sabah, probably not going to Iran. I will call Ali from my room."

Jack watched Sabah's eyes brighten and knew he was delighted that his friend may have a problem. An American with a problem in the Arab world is an opportunity. Jack was well aware of Sabah's delight in earning money from foreign businessmen and knew Sabah's retirement plan grew daily from solving problems for befuddled Western men. He had told Jack he prayed for the day when women and tourists would be allowed into the country; then he would become as rich as a sheik.

"You have room 435. The view is of the souk."

Jack palmed a ten-dinar note for Sabah's retirement plan and took the key. He grabbed his bag and headed to the upgraded fourth floor.

Room 435 smelled of dank sweat and French cigarettes. The window air conditioner rasped and shuddered, choking from desert sand fouling its coils. An orange, green, and red rug, knotted and gritty, partially covered the concrete floor. A single chair, a once-white table, one twin bed with a kit of two sheets, a pillowcase, and a ragged towel dressed the bed. Jack dropped his bag and turned the dial on an old Stromberg-Carlson twelve-channel television. Test patterns, a Chinese cartoon show, and Egyptian movies reminded him where he was.

The dialless black telephone perched on a table by the window connected directly to a gruff, strained male voice somewhere in the hollows of the hotel. "'Ello, Mr. Jack. Who do you wish to call at this hour?" challenged the night operator.

"I wish to speak to a friend in Tehran. Put me through to 98 021 921 9688."

"Moment."

The irascibility of Middle East telephone lines eased after midnight and before nine in the morning. On the second ring, Jack heard a familiar greeting. "If it is Mr. Jack, you are welcome, most welcome. The line has been kept open for you, and finally you have called. I'm the most important assistant to the honorable Mr. Mustafa Khaki. My name is Ali. You're the one who knows Farideh, his daughter?"

"Yes, I know her, and I know you. Why did you want me to call?" Jack was cautious. Ali was in a position to be an ally or an enemy.

"Well, you know Mr. Khaki is a powerful man ... has many friends who are also powerful."

"Yes, and what about Farideh? Is she okay?"

"Her father could get her out of Iran in a minute, but never mind. These are difficult times, and he wants to speak with you—not about Farideh, but about his other daughter, Leah. He thinks you can help, so he help you with business problems you left in this country. I know you had to escape when the Revolutionary Guard took the embassy. Some people owe you money?"

Ali's voice was lost, drowned out by static bleeps, hisses, zaps, and whistles that sounded like the background noise of a faraway radio station. Before Jack could try to reconnect, the phone rang. "Mr. Jack, I'm sorry; the line was disconnected, but I have it again and must talk fast. Boss wants you to come Iran now. He needs your help with medicine from the US. Leah has sickness; we have sanctions here, but she needs medicine so she can have dialsis."

"*Dialysis* it's called, for kidney disease."

"Yeah, that's it—dialsis. I've heard her say it. Doctors from America gave her medicine, big machine too. Come to Tehran under the protection of Mr. Khaki. Call me with flight details. I will personally meet you at Mehrabad Airport. Get different passport. American passport no good here now. You'll be killed if they think you're American. Be someone else."

ELEVEN

Baba Souk

I t could as well have been the Ides of March in 750 BC; nothing had changed in the Baba Souk in a thousand years. Twelve apostles could have strolled through the tented souk without drawing a glance. Less apostolic white-robed figures had roamed such undistinguishable old markets all over the Middle East since time was new. Salesmen, shouting in unmitigated exaggeration the exalted provenance of their wares, had learned their trade at their grandfathers' feet just as those grandfathers had learned it from their grandfathers. They stood under lazy wooden fans strung from bamboo poles and pummeled the passing crowds with promises of a better life if they would only buy their goods. Perfumed scents of oranges from the Lebanon blended with sticky sweet aromas of figs from the deltas of Basra and lemons from the Levant. Sweaty vendors stretched unclenched hands, one dripping red grapes, another bulging with wrinkled Egyptian dates. Wooden stalls were elevated a step or two above dirt floors that had been trampled by legions of flat wooden sandals with rope thongs that separated ugly big toes from ugly little ones. Women wore rubber flats, barely hiding fashionably painted toenails. They searched for camphor and eucalyptus oils to air their homes, trinkets for daughters, and cosmetics for private time.

Jack always enjoyed walking through the souk. He could find anything he wanted in the maze of the biblical bazaar. Today's mission, to buy a fake passport, had to be successful or he would not be able to buy an airline ticket to Tehran.

Among the weekend crowds, Jack muscled his way through heaving knots of sweating, stinking bodies heading for the money changers' tables in the crowded center of the bazaar. There, in a square of twelve shops elevated three steps above dirt floors, sat merchants whose self-importance placed them above the food and clothing peddlers and the gold sellers tucked in adjoining aisles. Behind each of their important stalls, loosely separated by dusty brown curtains, heavy safe doors were left open, tempting onlookers to value the wealth of the vendors' enterprise. The portly money changers busied themselves sliding abacus beads while calculating values of Iraqi pounds, Kuwaiti dinars, or the prized American dollar.

Bandar Al-Bandar and Company, founded in 1893 according to an overhead plaque, held the prominent center spot with a three-man staff of gray beards who had likely attended the souk's ribbon cutting ceremonies in the year one.

When Jack gave his reference, the man he had come to see stuck out his hand, beaming as if his camel had just given birth. Yes, he knew Sabah at Le Méridien, and yes, he would, with the blessings of Allah, do all he could for Jack Devlin and "his children's children, Allah be willing."

After exchanging pleasantries, welcoming each other to each other's presence, Jack said, "I need to buy a British passport."

"A foreign passport?" The rumpled look on his face suggested that neither Allah nor he would be willing. "My friend, where would I get such a thing? These are not bartered papers to be sold stall to stall. Impossible," he admonished.

Jack knew this was all a ruse and the man was merely considering how much money he was about to make. Al-Bandar was the right man. "Sabah said a British passport would probably cost fifty dinars," Jack said with conviction.

"As we say in Arabic, the man is *majnoon*—crazy. Never have I seen one—especially a British one—for less than one hundred dinars."

"All right, sixty."

"Seventy," he shouted over his shoulder as he pulled back the dusty curtain exposing the safe's faceplate, which illustrated a very foreign name shadowed in gold lettering: "Diebold Safe and Lock Co., Canton, Ohio."

Pretending astonishment, the son of the son of the original Bandar Al-Bandar held a fistful of passports. "*In'shal'lah*, it was only yesterday my friend asked me to protect these exceedingly rare treasures until his return from Baghdad. He had three: two English beauties and, here, a Swedish one."

Jack studied them, discarding the well-worn blue Swedish passport. Another had belonged to a smiling Englishman born in 1949—too young. The photo could be changed, but not the date. The second was an abused passport that read,

> BRUCE CHANDLER:
> DOB July 14, 1942
> Leeds, West Yorkshire
> United Kingdom

Perfect. "This one, my friend. Sixty-five dinars," Jack said, reopening the bartering. It was a game, and he loved it.

"My friend will scold me if I sell at even one dinar less, Mr. Jack. You will not find these rare treasures in another stall. You win; sixty-eight."

Smiling, Jack handed over the money and his passport photo. He had been prepared to spend a hundred dinars. In a few minutes, Bandar Al-Bandar returned, Jack's photograph ironed into the passport's first page, having replaced the photo of the curiously missing Bruce Chandler. The money changer and Jack bowed to each other in an honorific *metania*, muttering their good-byes.

Tucking Chandler's passport into a pouch under his shirt, Jack moved toward the cacophony of the street, passing three young ladies in black robes wearing Lone Ranger masks. Two had diaphanous black strips across their mouths as they shopped the sweets bazaars and the perfume souks. The black-robed women studied tables loaded with lipsticks for hidden lips, soaps that would not blur henna tattoos, and bottles of Breck shampoo to glisten hair that would never be seen by anyone except their mothers, girlfriends, and possibly their husbands.

Near the exit, fez-capped Nubians strolled, tilting long snouts of brass servers to pour lukewarm cardamom coffee into handleless cups for a small fee. Black Arabs from the tribes of West Africa, their faces ritually scarred, pitched to carry shoppers' bags for a few coins. An organ grinder with a monkey would not have been out of place, but an American in faded jeans was. The time had come to get on with his mission.

Jack Devlin never left the Baba Souk. Bruce Chandler did.

TWELVE

Tehran, March 1980

Kuwait Airways' waiting room for the early-morning flight to Tehran had all the odors associated with an early-morning bar except stale beer. The round-trip ticket to Tehran tucked into Jack's pocket bore Bruce Chandler's name. It was a kind of game for Jack to identify other passengers' countries of origin. Foreigners stood out; they wore shoes. Egyptians knotted atrocious plaid ties over wrinkled wash-and-wear shirts. Two Chinese men in Mao coveralls stood on the edge of assorted Arabs, Iranians, and a few Turks. Fragrances in the "males only" area suggested the presence of a small goat somewhere in the room, exhaling from both ends.

For his trip to Tehran, he took pains to look British. He found a silly tie—one depicting a dandelion in a green field—to go with a button-down blue shirt and rumpled gray pants. Brits were being allowed access to their soon-to-be-closed embassy. They did not dress up.

Jack had been awake since four in the morning, wrestling with rumors that Westerners attempting to enter Iran were shunted to windowless rooms, never to be seen again. That had pit-of-the-stomach impact. "What if I can't pull off the impersonation?" he asked himself while practicing Bruce

Chandler's Yorkshire accent—a task even Londoners would find difficult.

Waiting for the flight, Jack daydreamed. He had loved international situations since he was a kid, when he met his first foreigner—a Canadian college student visiting his school. Even though the Canadian was older—twenty-four, maybe—he did not seem so different. Jack had just stared at him intently, in silent awe, amazed the man's eyes were blue, his hair wavy, his posture, clothes, and mannerisms like those of Americans. Still, there was something about him—something foreign. In Jack's ever curious mind, and in the heart of his soul, he wondered what the Canadian thought, being in a strange land. Jack longed to see where the stranger lived, how he lived, what it was like to actually be in the man's house. He said it was outside Toronto, which sounded like an Indian word.

In the years since the foreigner dropped into class, Jack had been to countries from Argentina to the USSR, but he still had as much awe of foreign travel as he'd had back in the classroom at St. Peter's Central Catholic.

"Tehran, mate?" The questioner was a Scot. Only a Scot could put that many r's in "Tehran." He stood with a short, stubby countryman; both were in work clothes. "Or are you heading through to Kabul like me an' me mate?"

Jack liked Scots. They were jolly, loved to drink even if no one else paid, and were always ready for a fight.

The Scot stuffed a cigarette into his mouth.

Jack took another moment to assess both men. "No, just Tehran. Day trip, back tonight," he said with fervent hope.

The man finished lighting his pal's cigarette and said, "Sorry, chappy; like one? Tehran, eh?"

"No thanks. I'm in merchant banking; London is closing our Tehran office. Formalities won't take long."

"Well, we'll not even get off the plane to stretch our legs. Kabul is more civilized." He lit another cigarette from the stub.

Jack moved in the shuffle to climb the rear stairs of the Kuwait Airways 727. He sat on the aisle, next to a Persian mother and daughter, slid his overnight bag under the seat in front of him, and pretended to sleep. He had been an MI6 agent for less than a week but was already heading into the kind of danger he'd read about in Ian Fleming's books, except no beautiful women had turned up to take advantage of him. They played only in the late night of his imagination.

The flight, like the landing at Mehrabad Airport, was routine; he'd done it a dozen times. When the plane rolled to a stop at the terminal, the stairs lowered and passengers made their unruly way to the exits. Everything looked the same around the small terminal except for the absence of Pan Am ticket counters and signs. At this time of day, there would have been two Pan Am Boeing 707s next to each other on the tarmac. Pan Am flight 1 would be taking off for New York via London. Pan Am flight 2 would be flying in the opposite direction; its last Asian stop before New York would be Tokyo. Their around-the-world flight paths crossed at Mehrabad.

The terminal seemed little different than it had been before Ayatollah Khomeini turned the country upside down. Jack spotted a couple of fashionably dressed women accompanied by tieless uncles in dark suits wearing four-day-old beards heading for a flight to Paris. Mullahs and religious police looked over each departing passenger, caring particularly to check that Iranian men had not shaved. To do so would have courted the infidel version of vanity. In a few hours, the men's gray stubble would be covered in white shaving cream and whipped off before their nieces finished unpacking. Persian men honored the mullahs' harsh rules until out of Iranian airspace.

Mobs at another boarding area were dressed for their destination—Mecca, in Saudi Arabia. Men in white swaddling, one shoulder exposed, accompanied by unchristian numbers of women, were flying off to pay homage at the two holy mosques. The terminal bulged with pilgrims but was absent of Western businessmen. Months earlier there would have been hundreds, their leather briefcases stuffed with plans and projects.

A man slipped in front of Jack in the immigration line. His body odor gave him a pass; Jack let him in. He had not been on the flight. When the man reached the immigration desk, he snatched Jack's passport from his hand, shoving it in front of the officer. Jack's training kicked in. He would be patient, quiet, but ready to react if he was to be led away to the interrogation room. Then he caught a glimpse of the officer tucking something into his pocket after shaking hands with the foul-smelling man.

Thumbing the passport's pages, the officer studied Jack in silence. Whoever Bruce Chandler had been, his passport had several stamps for entry to Iran. The most recent was only a few months earlier. The officer continued to glare, and then, in a split second, he stamped the passport and waved him on. Jack had been admitted to the Islamic Republic of Iran.

Policemen loitered by the main exits; there were no revolutionary guards in sight. They would have stood out, their jugulars covered by black neckerchiefs, Kalashnikovs held close. The policemen were smoking and talking, paying little attention to the man walking ahead of Jack, or to Jack.

In the thinning crowd, expressionless officials watched him in silence as they did the few other Westerners moving toward a Lufthansa flight for Frankfurt. His tongue swished across the dry roof of his mouth when he pushed through the terminal doors and headed for the parking lot. The odiferous man followed him, motioned Jack toward a row of cars, and then walked off.

A black-gloved hand slapped him on the shoulder. "Salaam, Mr. Jack." Ali bore the look of a Turkish warrior. His build was solid, a couple of inches shorter than six feet. He had heavy legs and more than a fair share of hair. Jack remembered him. He was one of a thousand generic Turks in appearance, but one of a kind in ruthlessness. Ali led him through the lot to a Mercedes, opened his door, slammed it shut, and jumped into the driver's seat. He shouted at the car to start, honking the horn at no one in particular.

Ali slalomed out of the lot to a dead stop among other honking cars fighting their way into an intersection. Busses packed with workers joined the ragged procession heading to town, their drivers blowing louder horns, shaking fists, and shouting for Allah to strike dead every driver in their way. The blunt dissonance was routine. It would not be Tehran if cars, busses, and trucks were not armed with horns and angry drivers.

Ali took a select route to show Jack where power was lost. He drove to Roosevelt Street, which had been named in honor of the once special relationship between America and Iran. The mustachioed Turk said it was the only route. He lied. It was the route he selected to take his American passenger past the embassy of the United States.

Jack knew the area well; he'd had several meetings with commercial officers, many of whom would still be there, chained to pillars in the basement.

The Mercedes slowed, and Ali draped his arm over the seat back, resting his chin and coarse brown mustache on his forearm. "Embassy Amerikia," he grunted, wagging a thick finger toward the compound. "Hostages be there. Maybe killed now or killed later. I say kill now; nobody listen."

Jack did not look. He would not give Ali the satisfaction, but his heart throbbed in an anger that would focus his work. The hostages had to be rescued; he would do anything to make it happen. "Just the way it is, Ali. Politics. Ugly, right?"

Ali drove on, avoiding a military policeman's waving hand to slow down; he was speeding toward the wealthy suburb called Shemiran and his boss's compound. He drove the Mercedes like a tank, rolling through red lights, ignoring lane markers, cursing in Turkish, Farsi, and English. Upscale traffic in the Shemiran section of Tehran was jammed with Buicks and Cadillacs swapping lanes with Mercedes and BMWs. The drivers were punishing folded fists on dashboards, pounding horns, and decorating every window with single fingers.

"My boss likes you. His daughters like you. Other people here don't. You think he can help you get your money from the bank in Karaj—forget it. You're wasting time. Boss only wants you here to help stupid, sick Leah. Me and Mr. Khaki have huge deal to finish; no time for you."

Jack controlled his response. "How is she? Do you see her?"

"Only the boss, Farideh, and the nurse see her," Ali said. "They are getting information for you to buy dialsis parts. Then you must leave, go, get out of this country." He took his eyes off the road to look back. "Stupid sickness bad for business. I make money when Khaki does deals." The Mercedes slid across a lane, creasing the side of a small panel truck, raising no more than a "shit" from Ali.

At the T intersection off Pahlavi Road, Nasibi Street led to the arms dealer's compound, which was boxed within fortress-like walls. An ornate gate with a cop box on either side hid the ground floor from sight. It was all familiar; Jack had been to the home earlier to discuss Khaki's shipping interests in the port of Bandar Shahpur. The cover business was exporting rugs. His letters of credit were paid through the Bank of Karaj, and so were Jack's. He remembered Khaki to be bright, engaging, almost jovial; he seemed entirely comfortable with himself, commanding every meeting.

When they first met, months before the revolution, Khaki got to know Jack as a connected merchant banker and now believed Jack could get around import sanctions and arrange care and medication for his daughter. In the midst of the revolution, Khaki could leverage Jack by helping get his money, which was tied up in Gordian knots by Iranian banks—including the one he owned. It would be a typical Middle Eastern deal. Neither party had any idea what the other really wanted. Jack was after two treasures: Khaki's oldest daughter and his business ledger. Khaki wanted his daughters out of the way, out of his sight; they were an imposition on his time and resources.

Everything he had learned at MI6 would be put to the test the instant Ali dropped him inside the compound. Jack willed every ounce of his character to be calm, controlling his emotions. He was not afraid, remembering a comment from an old MI6 spy master who taught situational analysis. He had said, "Remember, Mr. Devlin: fear, in reasonable proportion, is your friend. Unreasonable fear comes from lack of planning. Planning will save you, save your mission; fear will eliminate both."

THIRTEEN

The Arms Dealer

A security guard, gun holstered on his hip, escorted Jack up marble stairs glistening in the warming sun. He pushed aside ten-foot-high glass doors that opened to Khaki's palatial office. Jack was to be received by the boss immediately.

Mustafa Khaki sat sweating in a raised chair behind a desk large enough to support a small enterprise. Khaki laid his pen on a notebook, pushed his chair back, and bounded toward Jack, smiling, praising Allah for returning Jack to his presence.

Perspiration on the broad expanse of his shiny forehead dribbled onto the collar of his sharkskin suit. Air-conditioning the man's office was a waste of money. Porcelain tile portraits of bygone dynasties graced the office walls. A wide arched window, its teal drapes corseted to brass hooks, outlined the view of Tehran, where dozens of minarets punctured the sky. On his desk, a three-inch-thick ledger lay open.

They embraced in a quick man-hug, providing enough time for Jack to feel for a gun or bulletproof vest. He found neither and acted quickly to avoid being overcome by Khaki's gardenia-scented cologne. The hug felt like an eternity. Jack stepped back and shook Khaki's hand, which felt like the sweaty palm of a pudgy kid.

The overstuffed Persian let go of Jack's hand and noisily dropped back into his chair. Behind Khaki, two burly Turks in rumpled black suits, guns bulging above their waists, bracketed Ali. All three had thick, coarse mustaches that looked as if they had been cut and pasted from the part of a horse's tail closest to its ass.

"Welcome, Mr. Jack." Khaki motioned to a chair. "You are welcome back to my home, young man. Sit here, my friend. I am so happy to see you back in Tehran and will protect you every minute. Had a nice trip, I suppose? Came up from Kuwait, yes? You are well known there, Mr. Jack; I have learned all about you. You have no secrets from me. I know everything."

Braggart, Jack thought. *Men like Khaki brag about what little they know—and everything they don't.*

"Regarding my dear daughter's health problems, she has to be stabilized so she can travel. I'm getting her out of this awful country soon; she needs medicine, and her machine is old. You will help?" It was an order in the form of a question.

Jack sat on the edge of the massive brown leather chair, eager to hear what else the smiling Buddha had to say.

Khaki rubbed his hands together, eyeing Jack from his elevated seat, and said, "I am sorry about our miserable behavior in taking over your embassy … bad, very bad. This mess will not end soon." He offered Jack a French Gitanes cigarette from a pack that was sitting on the desk next to a Russian Zorki camera.

One of the Turks poured tea from a gilded carafe into a thin, handleless cup—a thimble in Khaki's thick hand.

"I know why I want you here, Mr. Jack, but you have your own reasons. Tell me, what do you wish?"

If he really knew, I'd be dead by now. "There is a matter to be settled. My money was in the Bank of Karaj, your bank, when the Revolutionary Guard burned it down. Your insurance should cover my loss."

Khaki smiled, spread his hands, and said, "Yes, my bank killed several deals, including some of yours, to satisfy the revolutionaries. I'm very sorry you lost some money. I will do what I can to get some of it back for you."

Jack read Khaki's smile as sinister, believing it had been sinister from conception. Trivelpiece had warned that Khaki's manner would disguise his thoughts. If he discovered Jack's real motive, he would not let on.

Khaki was not the kind of man to be concerned with the piercing screams of neighbors dragged from their homes in the middle of the night or the slaughter of Shah Pahlavi's state officials in Evin Prison. Arms dealers have a way of sorting out their customers, whatever their allegiance. Guns have no loyalty. In the warlike relationship between survivors of the shah's government and the revolutionaries, Mustafa Khaki was never on the wrong side. He sold to both. In time, one or the other would turn on him. He would be devoured, and he knew it.

A Turk snapped a lighter for Khaki's Gitanes and resumed his lackey post. "Mr. Jack, your countrymen are suffering from Carter's failed policies just as we suffered under the shah. But these are matters for others; let us drink to your health."

Jack took the small glass of tea from a white-robed servant and offered a toast. "To your daughters, to Leah, and to Farideh."

Khaki banged the glass on his desk and then focused on his guest and grimaced. "You are aware, sir, I hate most Americans? They killed my wife."

Jack felt the bodyguards' evil eyes watching him for a reaction. He hoped they could not see the hair on the back of his neck stand up.

"Do you know how beautiful she was?" Khaki asked. "The memory of that lady represents the joy a father sees in his daughter. In my dear Leah, my youngest daughter, I am reminded every day. Her face is the likeness of her mother. Do you know how my wife died, sir?" Khaki's manicured fingernails drummed on the mahogany arms of his chair. "Did you know that the chauffer who drove my queen to her death in a booby-trapped car was a stupid Iraqi Shiite? But it was the car, sir; it was the car sent by your CIA to kill me. Perhaps you know those American CIA pigs?"

"Never met any of them, Mr. Khaki," Jack coolly replied as his temperature soared.

"Well, I fooled them. I sent my wife in the first car; I took another one. I sent my wife in that car because I thought the Americans would try something, but they could not fool me. I am much too smart for stupid Americans." He roared with laughter; so did the Turks.

Khaki remembered how his wife had delighted in telling him his daughters were Jews because she was Jewish. Her torment had fueled his hatred of her. Raging passion had tricked him into a marriage he did not want, although it justified a nightly parade of Russian ladies to his separate quarters. His daughters were no more than collateral damage.

Radical Muslims said Allah would not forgive Khaki for succumbing to passion and marrying a non-Muslim—a mistake to haunt him until the gates of paradise slammed shut in his face. He would be denied admittance.

The room went silent. Khaki swung his enormous chair around to look out the window. Jack could not see him over the back of the chair, but the Turks could. They remained silent. Khaki spoke without turning back. "I have been deciding to let you in on my secret. You will be dead before you can use it on me, but it may make you think again about my daughter." He spun back. "Her mother was a Jew. She told me after we got married. *After.*"

Khaki held up his empty cup, demanding more, regaining his serpentine sneer. "I want to make sure, beyond any doubt, Mr. Jack, you will get everything Leah needs to maintain control of her damaged kidneys until I send her to London or to the United States—Texas, maybe—to get her the best kidney money can buy."

"And I need to make sure, beyond any doubt, that I'll get my money back."

"Agreed," Khaki said as he clapped his hands together. "Agreed."

Jack tried to stay calm, look calm, be in command. He summoned his most authoritative voice. "Give me a list of the medications your daughter needs and a description of the dialysis equipment with the serial numbers. Also, I'll need to take photographs of the machine." He placed his MI6-issue 35 mm Minox camera on the desk.

"No photographs, Mr. Jack; it is against our religion. Write down what you need." Khaki's challenge was soft.

"Look, Mr. Khaki; I don't want to take any chances with her health. You want her moved, okay, but it won't be easy. We will need to be prepared. Is the dialysis machine German?"

Khaki nodded. "Yes, Fresenius."

"The medications will be packed and shipped in monthly through Oman," Jack said.

Khaki banged his fist like a gavel on the desk. "No, it is foolish, stupid idea. I want ten shipments at one time, not one ten times. Too risky. I insist, ten this month and another ten next month. Go to Frankfurt and buy two Fresenius machines. Your Swiss contact can help. All German companies will be out of Iran in a month; Swiss will stay. I want twenty sets of medicine in ten days, and the machines too. Money will be deposited to your American account by my overseas company." Khaki banged his fist on the desk again as if pounding an imperial seal.

Using a handful of tissues to wipe his sweating face, cursing between swipes, he said, "You know, Mr. Jack, this nonsense with the Revolutionary Guard will not end for a very long time. Your hostages may not survive."

The tension Jack felt erupted in anger, fueled by Khaki's arrogance. Jack placed both palms on the desk, leaned toward Khaki's bulging eyes, face-to-face, and asserted, "They are not my hostages, sir. They are my countrymen in service to the people of the United States. They are *your* hostages."

Khaki's frown tightened; his face flushed, his response predictable. "I have nothing to do with this mess, my friend. I am just trying to get by in a complicated world."

Information Jack had learned at MI6 flashed in his mind. Khaki was buying arms from Pyongyang for Malay rebels, in Russia for the Iranians, and in Damascus for Arafat and the PLO. *Right, just trying to get by.*

Khaki took a phone call, and his expression changed abruptly. He shouted something in Farsi and rushed out, stammering in English, "Sorry, Mr. Jack. Wait here."

The three Turks followed; one grabbed the cigarettes. The ledger on the desk remained open, next to Khaki's empty teacup. It was either a colossal mistake or a trap.

Jack palmed the Minox and bent over the white accounting pages with ten to twelve entries on each page. The Farsi script meant nothing, but he knew a ledger layout no matter the language. *This was too easy, too fast; it has to be a trap*, he thought while remembering what another old MI6 warrior had said: "Opportunity may surprise and quickly pass. Don't let it happen." He snapped a photo of a page, advanced the film, took another, and quit when he had twelve.

Within seconds of pocketing the camera, a heavyweight security guard pushed through the door in a rush. His jacket swung open, flashing a holstered gun. "Come with me, American."

Beads of sweat broke out on Jack's forehead. Seconds earlier, and the gun would have been out of the holster.

The guard's boots slammed on the marble stairs as he led Jack down to a candy-colored suite. It smelled like a hospital room and looked the part with its teal curtains, chain pulls, and waist-high bed. A warmth came over Jack when he saw a singular bright spot: a nurse standing at the foot of the bed—an angel in white holding her patient's hand. From the bed, Leah raised her head, her friendly smile welcoming him, her thin arms stretching for a hug.

"Leah, good to see you again."

"Oh, Jack, Farideh told me you would come. This is Màasha, my nurse. She is like one of the family."

The loud sound of her father's shoes slapping the staircase quieted everyone in the room.

"This man is here to help get your medications and supplies," Khaki said, barging into the suite.

"Thank you for helping me," she whispered, gazing at Jack.

The nurse moved to a tall white cabinet. "Some of what we need is here, but we are running out," said Màasha. "I will write down the specific medications. We are worried about war and the sanctions; if we lose contact with Germany and cannot get supplies, we'll be lost."

"Can't you get these things locally?" Jack asked.

"The stuff available at Masih Danehvari Hospital is for peasants. It is from China or someplace," said Khaki. "That's why I brought you here."

Khaki patted Leah's head, stepped back, and said, "Mr. Jack, you may take pictures of the machinery, the supplies, and"—he paused to pick up a coil of tubing—"the medications on the table. I will use my camera to take the personal photos of Leah's body with her tubes connected. Wait outside. Nurse, draw the curtain." He turned. "Give me my camera," he demanded of the Turk waiting in the hallway.

When flashbulbs stopped popping, Khaki opened the curtain and said, "Okay, Mr. Jack; you may now take your pictures."

Jack held up a steady finger. "I need to put in a fresh roll of film." He took the camera out of his pocket, looking clumsy, as if unfamiliar with the small Minox.

Khaki grabbed the camera, took it in his pudgy fist, and laughed. "I think you just took a picture of your foot." He rewound the roll, opened the back of the camera, took out the film, and tossed the camera back to Jack. "I'll get this developed fast. I know you will have some wonderful memories and pictures of Iran. Ali will take care of it."

Silently Jack trembled, thinking how he would be dismembered, one joint at a time, if Ali saw the pictures of the ledger. "No need to trouble you, Mr. Khaki; I will have the best people in the States take care of my film and yours." He held his palm open. "Don't want to take any chances with my souvenir pictures or the ones of the medical supplies."

"Okay, put in your new roll and take your pictures; then we will have three rolls to develop. I'll keep this one for now." Khaki slipped the roll into his pocket.

Jack's mouth became as dry as the desert sand. He quickly loaded the roll of film, took pictures of the medical equipment and supplies, and stepped back into the hallway.

Khaki motioned to Jack to follow, the bodyguards a step behind. "Sorry, I have to leave—another engagement."

"Wait. I need all three rolls of film to get to my courier."

Khaki stopped and inclined his head. "Okay. Here, take everything."

Jack let out his breath when Khaki threw the Zorki and the roll of film to him.

"You will be taken to the riding club to meet Farideh, who will host dinner. As you know, she is a lawyer, but we can't afford her," Khaki chuckled. "Here she is now," he said, stopping at the office door.

Farideh descended the marble staircase to the silent attention of all five men. Her polished black platform boots enunciated every step. She wore a white pantsuit accented by a long strand of black pearls. Jack felt his heart jump but was careful not to show his feelings. She carried a chador, her head slightly bowed, honoring tradition by acknowledging only her father. She did not acknowledge Jack; his greeting would have to wait. The honorific paid, Farideh nodded again toward her father and exited toward the vestibule. Her presence and bearing had drained the room of any further discussions about business and medical supplies.

Jack diverted his eyes and stilled himself, counting the hours until they would be alone.

"We are finished here, sir; I am leaving for my lawyer's office. I will see that he completes the payment to your account. Your return flight to Kuwait is arranged for tomorrow. My people at the airport will look out for you. Work fast; I want these supplies immediately. Understand?" The squat man filled the doorway as he exited, the Turks on his heels.

Farideh returned wearing the chador and motioned to Jack to follow her. She walked past amber-stained bookcases, their shelves lined with antique treasures of porcelain ceramics. On a coffee table, an engraved museum book lay open to a page about Persian art. She pointed to the page and stopped by a hanging portrait of a woman, painted on glass. "A nineteenth-century Qajar," she said. It could have been her grandmother.

They were completely alone. Jack moved to embrace Farideh.

She pushed him back. "Why haven't I heard from you? You only called once."

"I tried. All calls to Iran are blocked." Jack took a step back, feeling rebuffed but knowing he wasn't. "I've missed you terribly, but right now we need to talk. There have been changes to our plans."

Her face tensed; color drained from her cheeks.

"No, not with us, Farideh. The changes will help us to escape Iran together. An old friend who's in the CIA agreed to help us. He has a powerful role in American and British intelligence in the Middle East. He has promised to use all the assets he has to get you out of the country—Leah too. In today's Iran, your father can't do it alone."

"Jack, I can't believe it."

"Well, there is a catch. In return I must deliver your father's ledger to them. The entire ledger."

Farideh turned ashen. "Impossible. You'll be killed. Me too. How could you agree to such an insane deal?" She stepped back.

"I want to get you and your sister to Europe, where Leah can get the medical help she needs, and where you and I can be together. But that can only happen if I get the ledger to the people helping us. I can't do one without the other."

Farideh appeared mystified.

"Are you okay?"

"I'm okay, Jack. Sure, I'm okay. Your deal means we will be condemned to death, but yeah, I'm okay."

"Farideh, it is our best chance; and I will be protecting you," he said as she leaned into his arms.

She narrowed her eyes. "There is no way we can take the ledger." She shook her head. "You're asking for the impossible."

He tightened his arms around her. "We will do this together. You're strong and focused. You and I will take care of Leah; we'll get her to England or France."

"How?"

"I don't know yet, but I'm going back to Kuwait to get the plan going."

She took his hand and walked toward the heavy drapes covering the windows. "Jack, we can't talk about this now. Someone might hear."

Farideh's radiance was as welcoming as her smile. She was the reality of every dream Jack had ever had. "Farideh, you are amazing. I know I'm asking you to risk your life, but I will protect you."

"I believe in you, in us, and I trust you."

The chador rustled as she walked to the door, locked it, then turned to Jack. She smiled, stepped out of her sandals, and let the chador fall to the floor. It was not the traditional three-piece outfit. Two were shoes.

The Shaki Riding Club, called the SRC among the city's bluebloods, was nestled in an ayatollah-free zone in the ritzy Tehran neighborhood of Shemiran. The club still hosted a few dealmakers and Tehran's elite, as it had for years. Months into the revolution, it was the only safe place for Farideh to have dinner with Jack. He arrived a few minutes early and spotted a couple of sloppily dressed business types going into the locker rooms. They were speaking Russian. He heard French, Arabic, and a little English from other guests and was disheartened, knowing that Ayatollah Khomeini would soon rid the country of all foreigners. Jack loved the country and hoped that Iran would return to its prerevolution glory.

The French maître d', in a white jacket and black bowtie had a pencil mustache that could have been drawn with a yellow number two. His pasted-on smile twitched. "Sorry, monsieur, members only."

"Mr. Khaki's assistant booked a table," Jack said. "Nice mustache."

The mustache stretched to a scornful smile under squinty eyes. "But of course; you are the first to arrive." Papers on his podium continued to be more important than eye contact. "We seat our most dignified guests in the dining room. However, as you must be British or English, the bar will be more to your liking."

"Right. Geography must have been your favorite subject in school."

The maître d' walked Jack to the far end of the lounge, past an overweight couple smoking cheroots while engaging the bartender in drivel. An old man in a vested, wrinkled gray suit, tieless, his shirt buttoned to the neck, sat alone on the last stool. On the rim of the bar, his elbows propped age-scarred hands cupping his worn and nearly hairless head. Bags under his gray eyes drooped like dried plums above an ancient moonscape nose and the gray stubble of a spotty beard. Without moving his hands, the old man tilted his head, glanced at Jack, and dropped back to whatever sorrowful reverie justified his large whisky.

Jack took a table for two near the end of the bar and ordered a French Bordeaux wine. He drifted into thoughts about Farideh—how she intrigued him, made his muscles taut, tempted him without even being in the same room. He knew of no other woman with such presence. Amid the restrained atmosphere of the new Iran, her joie de vivre stood out. Every ounce of her featherweight body was exquisite. When they touched, her body melted into his. Farideh had the intelligence of a scholar, the playfulness of a schoolgirl, and the determination of a commander. No description of her fine face, her perfect figure, or her regal bearing could be captured in mere words unless by a spiritual Persian poet.

The waiter placed a bucket on a stand next to the small table and said, "This is quite a rare French Bordeaux you have chosen. We only have a few left. Shall I wait for your guest to open it?"

Jack nodded; he would indeed wait. He thought about the day he first met Farideh, poolside at a resort on the Caspian Sea. It was a protected playground for the diplomatic corps, important foreign businessmen, and prosperous Iranian men treating guests to weekends at the seaside. He remembered precisely where he was sitting when conversations hushed, heads turned, and an exotic woman emerged from the dressing rooms. She wore a sheer pomegranate-red kaftan over a man-trap bikini and walked alone to a chaise lounge, two to the right of his. The men around the pool, from teens to twilighters, followed her steps in awe. Women stared with the stealth searching he knew they applied when assessing another woman for a fault, a flaw, or, at least, a pimple. They would find none.

A female staff member followed with folded towels, placed two on a side table, rolled a third into a pillow, and moved to stand behind the goddess. Hushed tones became silent when the attendant caught the kaftan and the goddess gracefully stretched out on the chaise lounge. A pool boy placed an oblong bowl of green and red grapes, oranges, and yellow bananas to her left and adjusted the umbrella. The crowd slipped back into their dreams of what might have been.

Reaching for a piece of fruit, she caught Jack's wandering eye. Slowly she peeled an orange, her eyes fixed on Jack.

"English?"

"American."

"I'm Persian."

"I'm Jack—Jack Devlin." His eyes flitted to her tan line.

"I'm Farideh Khaki. You may have heard of my father. He owns banks—Mustafa Khaki. It is his name that attracts all this silly attention. Fruit?"

Jack swung his legs off the chaise to face Farideh. "Sure," he said, reaching across the empty lounge between them for a handful of grapes. "My business is merchant banking. I deal with his bank."

"I don't know much about his business. Sometimes I feel I don't know my father; he makes me nervous."

She sounded as though she wanted to believe her father had a good side.

"Fathers are supposed to make their daughters feel loved."

Her voice softened. "He did when I was little."

Jack slid over to the unoccupied chaise between them, triggering more hushed whispers from the loungers around the pool. "If your father is very important, you must be the reason."

Farideh blushed.

"What do you do?" Jack asked.

"My degree is in common law. Sharia law is ancient and repressive thinking. Outside"—she nodded her head toward the street—"you and I could not even speak. I would be covered head-to-toe by a hijab and a chador."

"Have you thought about leaving?"

"Everyone is leaving. Most of my friends have gone to Paris. Still, I don't want to go. My sister, Leah, has a serious disease. I can't leave her. I need my father's permission. He insists he will make the arrangements when the time comes." Farideh looked around to see whether anyone was eavesdropping. "I'm so afraid that soon we will never be allowed to get out."

"Tell me about your happier moments when you were growing up."

"When I was fourteen, life was magical. We went to New York, stayed at the Waldorf Astoria. My father took me to a Broadway musical—*Annie*. It was just the two of us. Such a happy memory. You know one reason why? I could be outside without a head covering."

Jack watched Farideh relax into her memories and then prop up on an elbow, laughing.

"What's funny?"

"The next day, the hairstylist at the Waldorf completely ruined my hair—so badly that I had to wear a scarf to cover it up. Can you believe it?" Farideh laughed; she was enjoying herself. When her laughter settled, she smiled at Jack, who felt blinded, as if the sun had risen at midnight.

Farideh swiveled gracefully and bent down to put on her silk slippers.

"Maybe I could help you return to America—maybe next time to California." It was a statement more than a question.

Her face lit up. "That's quite an offer. Are you staying here, at the resort?" she asked.

"No, I'm at the Alborz Hotel."

"Tonight there will be a reception for the crown prince of Jordan. Would you like to join me for the reception and dinner? We would never be allowed to have dinner together at the Alborz; the religious police are everywhere."

Jack marveled at his good luck. "On one condition."

"What?"

"You let me tell you more about California."

She smiled. "Condition accepted."

In a fast round trip to the Alborz Hotel, he could shower, change, and be back in plenty of time for the reception and dinner with Farideh. He would take a toothbrush.

SIXTEEN

The Old Warrior

The old man at the bar stood tall, watching Pencil Mustache escort Farideh toward Jack's table. She brought the old man to full attention, a happy smile lighting her grandfather's face.

"Zayde," she exclaimed.

She was a lithe Venus clad in a long, flowing silk scarf of deep Caspian blue layered over an off-the-shoulder white chemise with white slacks and sandals. Hinting at the light blues of a Persian sunset, her silky blue head scarf mimicked a Persian twilight. Local women delighted in showing off Paris fashions within the privacy of the riding club. The old man enveloped Farideh in a grandfatherly hug, waving the Frenchman to the side.

Jack pulled out a chair for Farideh, but the old man's hands remained on her shoulders. In a raspy voice, he said to Jack, "Sir, I am General Marwan. Sorry to interrupt, but I must talk with Mademoiselle Khaki. It is a private matter." He spoke authoritatively. "Would you mind waiting in the lounge for a few minutes? Thank you." Advancing age had not lessened the strength of his handshake.

Farideh nodded. "It's okay, Jack; give me a few minutes."

The old general pulled out her chair and lifted her azure shawl to drape in cloud-like folds. Pencil Mustache picked up the wine bottle Jack had ordered and, in the uppity manner of a grand snob, lied, "May you both enjoy this most marvelous wine that I personally selected. It is a fine Mouton Rothschild Bordeaux. Phillipe Rothschild is a personal friend, and he has excellent taste." He held the bottle over the glass, tossing dismissive eyes toward Jack. Subtly, he winked at Farideh. His insufferable manner was ignored by General Marwan and Farideh but not by Jack.

Mustache deposited the bottle into a vintage silver bucket, ceremoniously wrapping a white napkin around its crest. "Come, Englishman. You will be waiting in the anteroom by the side door. *Allons y.*" He pirouetted toward the reception area.

Jack's reaction to Mustache was, so far, restrained because of an admonition he had learned in training. Trivelpiece had said impatience killed more intelligence people than guns, knives, or poison. He lectured him about discretion—a quality that usually evaded Jack. He would think about the chief's warning after the walk to the anteroom with Pencil Mustache.

The general got a pass; he was not the adversary of the interrupted evening. The old general had already fought and won his battles. His immediate battle was now directed at the ravages of time, and time was winning.

The maître d' would not get a pass. He did not bother to turn toward Jack when he opened a door to a small, dark anteroom. "Wait here," he said. "Wait—"

The sentence did not get finished. Jack's left hand clamped over the mustachioed mouth. His right hand bent Frenchie's arm back and up, between the shoulder blades, thrusting him against the wall. "My French isn't as good as yours, so I'll tell you in US of A English. Step out of line one more time and that mustache will be in your throat." Jack stepped back into the anteroom alone.

Another lesson Jack learned in his MI6 class on practical efficiency was that revenge does not need to be noisy and it does not need to take a lot of time. Jack had aced the course.

When he returned to the lounge, a waiter approached him cradling a bottle of champagne and said, "General Marwan sent his compliments and hoped you and Mademoiselle Farideh would enjoy this Dom Pérignon together with his blessing. He has paid the bill."

The bar was beginning to fill when Jack returned to Farideh. She spoke softly, telling him about her complicated family. "General Marwan is my *baba joon*—my dear grandfather. He gave me some bad news. Some of the far left have learned my father sold poison gas to Saddam Hussein. Their Russian friends are furious because it was theirs." Farideh shivered, pushed the champagne away, cupped her hands over her mouth, and said, "Jack, men are pigs. My father is a pig bastard—my own father."

Jack cradled her delicate hands in his. She pulled back a hand and wiped the wet mascara rolling down her cheeks.

"My grandfather said Leah and I must leave, and that a plan was being arranged to get us out. I'm worried about it, Jack. I told him you are also working on a plan for our escape and I can't tell Leah anything. She is so delicate; news like this would scare her to death."

Jack held her as she cried softly, and he then lifted her chin to look up at him. Their eyes locked. "Farideh, let your baba joon keep working on his plan. It might help. I'll let my guys know about it. You're not alone anymore."

Jack's plan for a romantic evening disappeared, love and romance set aside. He would step up plans to evacuate the ladies and advance his MI6 mission. "What about your father's head man, Ali?"

Farideh withdrew her hands and lifted an angered face. "Ali is a bastard too. He said he could ease Leah's path to Allah."

Jack took her hand and said, "Listen to me; look at me. If I can photograph the entire ledger, we can get you and your sister out. It's the only way."

"You are crazy. That can never happen. What do you mean? How will anyone see those pictures?"

"The canisters will be taken by courier on Kuwait Airways' parcel service."

Jack's voice had the kind of conviction Farideh needed. She would walk through any door Jack could open.

"Farideh, it'll be a long time before this country returns to the life you knew under the shah. President Carter was outsmarted by Khomeini, but hopefully Ronald Reagan will replace him. He will bring about change. We must understand Ali is not the only enemy to deal with. Russia wants to burrow into Iran, get close to top government people, and get the Iranians to depend on them for the security of the country. Then the Russian leprosy will devour your country from within."

"How do you know that? Who told you? It's not true. We'll never let anyone take over our country."

"You already have. The ayatollahs are the mice; Russia is the cat. The Russians will take a leadership role in Iran. Tribal wars will get worse from Baluchistan to Kazakhstan, and life will deteriorate all over the Middle East. Your Persia is gone; God help the new Iran. At least we have each other."

Farideh stared at him, looking confused. She used her knuckles in the delicate manner of a child, rubbing her eyes to wipe away tears.

Jack pressed his case with reason instead of passion. "What if we could neutralize your father's arms business, get your sister to a Western hospital, and ... help the Iranian people?"

"Neutralize my father? You want to kill my father?"

"No, he would not be killed; he would not even be hurt. It's simple. The ledger is never out of your father's sight, correct?"

"Unless Ali carries it for him."

"Get it to me for an hour and everything will be solved."

Farideh sat back as if pondering Jack's insane request. It was time for him to be quiet in the kind of silence he had learned about at MI6.

The wait was short. Farideh set her glass on the table. "Jack, I care for you. I love Iran, and I despise what my father does. I want him stopped, as you do, but are you thinking about me, Jack, or only about yourself, as he does? I've already offered to try to take some pictures, but now you want me to sneak the whole ledger out of the house and photograph every page? If I get caught, my father will kill me instantly. I know how he arranged my mother's death; my grandfather told me. It was Ali who planted the bomb in the car!"

"Farideh, I'm so sorry that happened to your mom. It's hard to believe anyone would do that."

"Ali would. He does what my father wants."

"So help me stop him." Jack's stomach was in knots; he was caught in a conflict. Farideh wanted a hero, not another nightmare.

Her expression changed. "I'm scared—not just for you and me but for Leah."

Jack raised his hand and looked around. "Careful; people listen."

"I'm so sorry. I do know you're thinking of me, of us—Leah too. But are we all going to die?"

"Absolutely not. You're going to be safe; I promise. Tonight I'm flying back to Kuwait to make the final arrangements."

Farideh gasped. "You can't just hop on a plane and fly back and forth like you did last year. You'll be arrested." Her hand covered her mouth.

"It will take me a few days to get everything in place."

"How?"

"I can't tell you how. Trust me."

"I do. I just want to know how you're going to get the ledger and us out of Iran."

He had no idea.

SEVENTEEN

Redirected to Cairo

J ack had no trouble leaving from Mehrabad Airport. His flight landed in Kuwait a few minutes before midnight. He scrambled through the airport quickly, dressed in jeans and a ragged brown sweater, carrying a gym bag. He fit in; no one paid any attention. He was almost out of the terminal when he felt a hand on his arm. A man in a tracksuit handed him an envelope.

"Hi, saw you in Moismann's belfry a couple nights ago with my friend, Eddie Furlong. He said you'd appreciate getting an update. They want you in Cairo."

"For what?"

"I don't know; something about a KGB defector. Egypt Air 617. You're booked at the Sheraton. Meet C for breakfast."

Jack's curiosity soared as fast as the exit of the tracksuit. He tore open the envelope. No letter, no explanations—just a plane ticket. The writing was legible through to the carbon. Egypt Air 617 would be at gate 23, departing at 2:00 a.m. He picked up his bag and headed for the gate.

The flight landed early, leaving plenty of time for Jack to get to the Sheraton. He knew the hotel well; it was in the heart of the city, part of an American chain. The ten-story Sheraton had two claims to fame: a belly dancer called Nadia Gamal, and its location next to the embassy of the USSR. He cleared immigration in twenty minutes, grabbed a cab, and sped through Heliopolis traffic, arriving in the city in time for his breakfast meeting.

Fava beans simmering in garlic and olive oil filled the hotel's dining room with the robust smell of *ful*, the most popular breakfast dish in the Arab world. Jack took a table on the far side of the ornate room near the "Garden of Sultan," ordered an American coffee, and wished in vain for an English newspaper.

Jack was early; he expected Trivelpiece would be on time. For C to come to Cairo meant the assignment had taken on greater urgency. The canisters of film with twelve pages of Khaki's ledger would have already been analyzed by MI6, and Trivelpiece would surely remind Jack he would have to do better, get more pictures—get the whole book.

He felt a stirring in the room. Arabs and Westerners looked up from their plates; heads turned toward the entry. An exquisite brunette in a Western business suit was searching the room. The Arab and Western heads swiveled back into place when the woman spotted Jack and moved toward his table. It was Pandora Quince.

He was shocked but rose to receive a brisk kiss on each cheek. The surprise he felt brought back the memory of his silent astonishment when he concluded she could walk. Elegance and cunning singled her out not just among agents but also against any group of men or women.

"Would you have preferred Plentiful Agatha?"

As she stood in the early-morning sunlight filtering through the garden's regal palms, Jack felt anticipation morph into intense curiosity. "Seeing you is always a special pleasure." His attempt to have a little conversation before ordering failed. Her cold expression indicated that she wanted to get down to business.

"Your job was to get the entire book." Pandora beckoned to a waiter. "Gahawa, ithnan."

Her Arabic was good enough to get them both coffee.

"You wanted me to come to Cairo so you could tell me what I already know? Good teachers never have to repeat the lesson they taught."

"True, if the student is good enough. There is only success and failure. Failure is anything other than the whole ledger. Do you think of yourself as a failure, Jack?"

The instant surge of pride that fell over Jack disappeared when his thoughts flipped to the urgency of his personal mission.

"I want to move on, Jack. You were told to come here for a different reason." From the inside pocket of her suit, Pandora took out an envelope. "Here is an unredacted abstract from a Russian microfiche reviewed in Washington, London, and both embassies in Moscow. It came from that KGB guy who wants to defect. The guy is here for a debriefing before his posting to Kuwait. He is part of Russia's Middle East Unit. He gave microfiche to an American agent in Moscow last week. It's about Russia's involvement with Iran and an operation intended to get the hostages removed from your embassy."

Pandora paused, allowing Jack time to glance through the abstract.

Jack handed the paper back. "So what does this have to do with me?"

"A car is waiting to take you to the British embassy, where you will be given an 'eyes only' report about the KGB agent. It arrived yesterday from London in the diplomatic pouch. It looks like he is out for himself and is defecting to get to the States. However, he could still be working for the KGB. Never trust a Russian."

"Shouldn't we talk somewhere more private?"

"No. The world doesn't care what people talk about, and we draw more attention when we hide meetings. Two of our local agents are over there, at the table near the fountain. They'll let me know if we are spotted. In fiction, agents meet on street corners; in real life, we are real people. Let's continue. The KGB fellow told the American agent he had vital information about the USSR and Iran. He said the Iranians are bending to a Russian plan to move the hostages."

"What's the surprise? That makes sense. The whole world knows the US will try to rescue our people. How could we not?"

Pandora agreed, adding, "It would be difficult with all the hostages in one place. Split them up and the degree of difficulty escalates to the impossible."

Jack finished his breakfast, waved for the bill, and then posed his question again. "What are you asking me to do?"

"Two things specifically. First, absorb the info you will be given at the embassy about Vladimir Sudakov, the KGB guy. He is also called the Translator. Second, come back to this hotel and go to room 317. From there you will have a clear view of the gardens in the Russian embassy. The hotel was built a few years ago, so the Russians should have moved then, but for some reason they did not. Three cheers for our side. At 3:00 p.m., Sudakov's boss, Vice Consul Yevgeny Primakovski, goes out for his daily walk. He is responsible for all KGB operations in the Middle East. We will be watching to see if Sudakov accompanies him. We want you to be able to recognize him when you meet."

"Meet?"

Pandora ignored the question. She picked up the creamer, hesitated, and said, "Sorry, I forgot; your file said you like your coffee black."

Pandora kept talking. "Primakovski is twice Sudakov's age and half his size. Your additional assignment, which we know you can handle, will be to work on Sudakov until he is extracted. That means you'll be responsible for getting two kinds of information out of him."

"Two kinds?"

"Yes. All the information he wants to give us and all the information he does not want to give us. Two kinds."

Jack had a picture in his mind of nails being hammered into a coffin—his.

"**S**udakov, you are an imbecile."

Vladimir Sudakov sucked in his breath and steadied himself, sure he had been discovered.

"These translations make no sense. You must demand better from your team."

Sudakov ducked when his boss threw the papers onto his desk. He turned back to the blank walls of his cubicle and leaned into a desk fan, trying to cool his panic. Days felt like months, the fear of exposure fraying every last nerve. There had been no contact since he met the American agent in Slovetsky Park. Maybe he gave away too much information too soon. Maybe the Americans had decided they no longer wanted to meet him. Maybe he should have stayed in his old job, running the translators' program at headquarters, and not taken the promotion to Kuwait.

He turned up the fan, sat back in his chair, and remembered the routine in Moscow. Every morning at six o'clock, Sudakov had watched thirty men walk down two flights of cold stone stairs to the subbasement of KGB headquarters. The men dressed alike in dark, scratchy wool clothing that blended with their grim pallor, which would not improve even when the sun returned to Moscow. Sudakov followed them at a fair distance, guided by rancid body odors and clomping work boots.

The translators never looked up; they ignored the automaton guard they passed daily. He unlocked an industrial door to a long, narrow gray room where fifteen wooden tables were anchored along one dirty whitewashed brick wall. Four-foot-long benches stood in front of each table. Above the tables were shelves. File boxes of newspapers and magazines to be translated sat on the top shelf, and stacks of paper sat on the lower shelf, at eye level. The room had once been a shooting range, used occasionally with enemies of the people trembling as targets against the cold brick walls.

One by one the men marched past the guard into the narrow room, single file; they had no choice. They hung their greatcoats on sturdy pegs opposite relegated positions and took their seats, two to a bench. Silence stilled the men who sat rigid, staring at the wall in ritual preparation for another dull day.

Each translator was a university graduate; some had master's degrees. Russian was their mother tongue; fluency in a second language their reason for being. Not one had applied for the job; nor could they have imagined that their brilliant academic careers would drop them into a tube-shaped room like puppets. These were not simple-minded, backward peasants. Many were graduates of Moscow Academy, which operated under the commanding patronage of the KGB. A few held degrees from Moscow University on Sparrow Hill. All espoused the motto of the KGB:

>Loyalty to the party
>Loyalty to motherland

Sudakov admired the translators. Their brilliance lay in proven abilities to translate syntax, nuance, and meaning in articles published in foreign newspapers and magazines, as well as in documents purloined from foreign embassies. The translators worked in dozens of languages, writing summaries indexed to the analyzed treatises. Their work was vital, providing KGB officers with the news of the world, including wrong-headed opinions of the USSR.

Sudakov scuffed his heavy boots as he paced the chamber, monitoring the progress of each translator. He did not speak to them; it was not part of his job description. Every couple of hours he reached over their shoulders, snatching the summaries collecting in low wooden boxes at each translator's place. The only other sounds in the hollow echoes of the room came from the tearing, crunching, and discarding of the analyzed papers.

"Comrade Sudakov!" shouted an officer—one of the two overseers—standing at a rostrum at the end of the room. The sound ping-ponged in the chamber, the last decrescendo syllables rippling. "Stop pacing; you are disturbing the others. Pay attention. Be silent."

"Idiot," Sudakov mouthed. *I am silent.* He leaned against the doorframe and decided that zippering his parka would be the limit of rebuttal. There was not any misconception in his understanding of the futility of challenge in the USSR. The smartest people got the worst jobs, and the worst people got the best jobs. He would stand still and wait until the next batch of summaries was ready. Waiting was the national pastime.

Ordered silence or not, he still would not speak to the Armenian on bench number three, whom he knew from the class they had shared in Arabic studies. He would not acknowledge the tall man from Tbilisi, a friend from Komsomol days who was probably a liar anyway. He had once told Sudakov that his family knew the Stalin family— said they were neighbors in Gori. *If he is so well connected, why is he stuck here translating Georgian?* He liked Vasily and wished they could share a beer and a smoke. But Vasily was responsible for American English, and he was watched by a surveillance team from the center at all times—wary that he might learn too much.

Sudakov constrained his disgust at the government for consigning bright young men to tedious work, day after day, in unforgiving cold in the cellars of KGB headquarters. For the rest of their miserable lives, they would sit on the wooden benches for ten hours a day, translating documents. Russia needed to know what the world was saying.

Sudakov lit a stinky Bulgarian Opal, threw the wooden match on the concrete floor, and dared to walk toward the two officers. "Comrades, it is time to bring the Farsi translations and the American translations, only those, upstairs. You know who ordered them. Shall I tell the chief translator you refused?"

Both officers looked up. One, tilting the black bill of his dull cap and folding his arms across his chest, said, "I can have you sent to a gulag today for making stupid statements. You will have the summaries when they're ready. These worthless peasants are too slow; I will send them to the gulags with you, moron."

"Mikhail," said his fellow minder, placing a strong hand on his partner's forearm, "the Farsi and American summaries are done. Give these to the idiot; he is only the second assistant translator—a delivery boy."

Sudakov tore the files from the officer's hand, slapping his heels in a return insult, and started up the cold stone steps, sidestepping the snow and ice left by sixty boots. In the basement of KGB headquarters, snow on stairs didn't melt until summer, and summer never came. Sudakov believed the sun only shone in the West.

"Delivery boy" stung; so did "imbecile." "Worthless" had been overused, and "idiot" was laughable. Why did Russia treat fellow Russians as if they were enemies and not assets? Why didn't the bosses appreciate how bright he was—how important to the cause? In KGB training, recruits watched grainy films of Western decadence—documentaries that condemned America's slavery of blacks and Wall Street greed, showing that there were fancy cars for some, run-down tenements for most. The films were followed by lectures about the virtues of spying on one's neighbors and their families. It was considered heroic to tell the authorities about negative whispers, even if the whisperer was a parent, a sibling, or a spouse. It was the duty of every Russian to turn dissenters in.

When he was a boy, he had cheered the Communist crushing of the Prague Spring and the KGB's heroic accomplishments in turning foreign agents. He had cheered Yuri Andropov's speeches to the Committee for State Security. But no one in the Committee for State Security, the KGB, and certainly no one in the Politburo cared or even knew that Vladimir Sudakov existed.

He realized he'd walked two doors past the microfiche department. It was risky to be even one door away from his assigned stop. Except for her physical presence, the office secretary's mind was elsewhere, oblivious to the long ash from her lipstick-smeared Opal. Even she did not notice Sudakov. Stacked on the reception desk, a black velvet bag held five canisters of the previous day's work in microfiche; one would be labeled simply "IRAN."

Sudakov dropped off the new summaries, shouting at the secretary, "Have these ready for tomorrow." He picked up the velvet bag as usual, but alone in the hallway, he quickly replaced the contents of the IRAN canister with an old tape he had pinched from the archives section. Sudakov's imagination glowed in the recognition that he was trading a canister of secrets for a dacha on a beach in the US. It would be so simple.

NINETEEN

British Embassy, Cairo

I n the Cairo office of the British embassy, a uniformed clerk showed Jack into a private conference room at the top of a flight of red granite stairs. The clerk spoke in hushed librarian tones. "You will not be disturbed, sir. I will see to it."

Jack kept his eyes on the clerk as he backed out of the room. The room had the feel of an English library. Heavy, ornate ten-foot-high drapes blocked natural light but not the raucous sounds of crowds in Tahrir Square. The russet-brown oak panels separating the windows held framed pencil-drawn likenesses of Winston Churchill and Prime Minister Callaghan. Jack was mesmerized by a richly woven colorful tapestry on the opposite wall. He silently chuckled, thinking only the Brits would so prominently display Sudanese warriors bludgeoning Egyptians and throwing their headless bodies into the Nile.

The manila folder was fastened with a pompous seal. The black-bordered label read "Top Secret, Agent J. D., Eyes Only." He was alone in the room. The reality of the clandestine world was settling in.

The file was from the master spy himself, Algernon Trivelpiece. MI6 had received a request from the CIA to validate a rogue KGB agent. The Russian's name: Vladimir

Sudakov. MI6 would determine whether Sudakov met the definition of "actionable value." Trivelpiece's note said he had advised Washington that his Cairo MI6 office was swamped, so a new man, Agent Jack Devlin, would be responsible for matters relating to Sudakov and would report directly back to him.

The boundaries originally agreed on with Hugh Ebanks and Pandora Quince were being stretched. Their names were not mentioned in the file, but they had to have given their support to the additional mission. The only person who had not been consulted was Jack himself.

A personal note Trivelpiece attached to the file said the Americans would hesitate to work with a presumed Russian turncoat. "Agent Devlin, if you become convinced of Sudakov's value and we can verify his information, the Americans would owe MI6 a return favor. I would be personally indebted to you for that."

Jack looked up at the portrait of Winston Churchill; his pensive and commanding presence endorsed the inference of Trivelpiece's message.

Jack thumbed through the papers to get a feel for the Russian. At once he found the subject interesting. Sudakov was described as a fumbling academic of privileged birth, smart enough to learn Arabic and clever enough to bust out of the pool of Komsomol students and into the ranks of the KGB. There were three pictures of the target. One was a class photo; the student circled was Sudakov. The other two were candid shots, more recent; neither one gave a clear view of the Russian's face, but his bulk was evident even in the class photo.

The dossier said Sudakov's father had served Molotov and Stalin, which meant his son was brought up in luxury, attended the academies, and had perks other Russian boys could not hope to have. The file described him as a marginal KGB agent—not ready for promotion, limited to political espionage. There were no positive comments, but background reports mentioned excessive drinking and partying. Excessive drinking would not distinguish him from other Russians.

He read the file to its conclusion. Sudakov was being transferred to Kuwait and would take up his post after debriefing in Cairo. Trivelpiece believed Sudakov could be more an asset than a liability, and Agent Devlin would be his proxy to find out.

> Mr. Devlin,
>   Confirm Sudakov, strip him clean, and get all his information—everything he has. You might gain access to information that would affect Khaki, even your girl, Farideh.

Trivelpiece's sign-off was in character:

> Hope if anyone gets killed as this plays out, it won't be you. Best of luck. And, Mr. Devlin, be careful.
>
>   C

"Thanks, Chief," Jack mumbled.

He felt he had been given keys to a sanctum of secret files as he studied the two sets of translations of the microfiche data—one by the British experts and another by the Americans. Differences in the translations were unambiguous, the summaries parallel and mostly inconclusive—except for one important section that gave him an adrenaline rush.

Both translations said the Russians and Iranians would move the hostages to a remote prison near the Azerbaijan border, where they would be killed by Azerbaijan regulars. Once the hostages were dead, Iranian troops would execute the Azerbaijanis and proclaim they had exacted revenge on behalf of the Americans. Iran would be off the hook, and Russia would have a new friend. The second plan, less favored by the Russians, would keep the hostages alive but disperse them to separate locations around the country.

Jack's stomach churned; his anger throbbed. Russia's plan would solidify its ties to Iran; they would get access to warm-water ports and other concessions, and fifty-three Americans would lose their lives.

"Those bastards."

The need for action was immediate, so why had MI6 waited until he got the file? What did this have to do with Khaki?

He skipped the taxi rank. In Cairo's traffic it would take less time to walk back to Pandora's hotel. He found her in the garden reading Kahlil Gibran.

"If Gibran has answers for you, I want to read it next."

"Here's an answer for you, Jack: The Russian's information is crucial to protect the American hostages. We need to learn how much they control Khaki. They say they own him—why? Sudakov is valuable to your side and to ours."

"Don't lose sight of my mission, Pandora. I want Farideh out."

"We'll see to it, Jack, one step at a time. Right now we'll try to figure out how to squeeze the KGB agent."

TWENTY

Walls Too Short

J ack could not wait to see what Vladimir Sudakov looked like in person. His focus on Sudakov changed when he stepped out of the Sheraton elevator and saw a maid closing the door of room 317. "Ahlan wa sahlan," he said.

"Ahlan bik," she responded with a hint of a smile.

"Enta Sudanani?" he asked, guessing that she, like most hotel maids, was from the Sudan.

"Nam, Dinka," she replied cheerfully. "Yes, I'm of the Dinka tribe. You speak my language?"

Not very well, he thought, *or you wouldn't have asked the question.*

The Dinka maid was as hospitable as if she oversaw sales. "Would you like to see this room?" She opened the door and showed him the view, pointing out a sculpture garden. "Russians go there. Maybe Russian company. Maybe big *sherekat*." She closed the floor-length drapes and spun around to look at Jack with a Sudanese smile that could capture an entire regiment.

"You speak my language very well," he said.

Her Nubian facial features were like those of European women rather than the thick-lipped, broad-nosed look of the West Africans. Their radiance was celebrated in bars from the Red Sea to the Sahara. Her cheeks had facial scars, which identified her as belonging to one of the tribes living on the banks of the Blue Nile.

"Room free now, no booked, already cleaned." She took the tip Jack offered, tucking the Egyptian pounds into her apron. The maid's hand rested on the doorknob; her slim body edged to open it a little. Jack felt an invitation. She gestured for Jack to give the room a second look, then humbled her eyes toward the floor, her free hand turned to the side. The light tan skin on the inside of her hand contrasted with her ebony body.

Jack stared at her thin nostrils and fine lips and felt the elegant calmness that proclaims femininity and befuddles men, weak or strong. He felt silly, like a boy sneaking a peek at a copy of *Playboy* on a magazine rack in the drugstore. Jack straightened his shoulders, stiffened the rest of his body, and embraced his ability to pretend. She was not Farideh. He used his sleeve to blot the surge of sweat on his forehead cooked up in a hot hallway by a hot maid.

Giggling, she stepped into the hall, waved, and said, "Bye bye."

Jack went to the window. He was to expect two men to enter the embassy garden. The younger and bigger man would be Sudakov; the other, his boss, Vice Consul Yevgeny Primakovski. Other pictures in the file he had reviewed at the embassy showed Sudakov's boss. One was a head-and-shoulders shot, and one was of Primakovski at the Kremlin wall, standing behind Brezhnev.

According to the file, Sudakov had worked for the vice consul in Moscow on the Middle East desk. Both spoke fluent Arabic, both had graduated from Moscow Academy, and both worked on the USSR's interests in the region. Vice Consul Primakovski's cover was agronomy. He belonged to the upper ranks of the KGB. Sudakov served as cultural attaché. He would belong to Jack.

Desert heat, borne on the winds, relentlessly overcame the hotel's best efforts to cool down. Room 317 was at the far end of a long hallway; it caught the full brunt of heat from the wind tunnel effect. Hugh Ebanks blew in with the wind wearing a white dishdasha, rivulets of perspiration glistening on his face. He looked like a Nubian royal. "Didn't expect to see me, Jack? No surprises in this business—none."

"Okay, here's a surprise for you. Get me back on the track to get Farideh out or forget the ledger," Jack said, looking Hugh up and down.

"Relax, Jack, I'm on it. You're wondering why I dressed like this? Ha! I would have been the only black guy wearing a suit in Cairo."

"You look good in those white robes. Try them at Langley."

Upset or not, Hugh was a touch of home for Jack— someone he liked, a person he believed could be trusted. But Hugh had changed. He was not the same guy from years earlier when they worked on ships, where they had built a bond based on trust and an unexpressed, deeply felt understanding that their souls were the same color. Neither Jack nor Hugh ever said out loud that he trusted the other. It was implicit in the silent awareness that they could finish each other's sentences, thrived on challenges, and came up with the same solutions to problems. Jack made up his mind to give Hugh every reason to verify their old bonds— especially their bond of trust. He was sure he would.

Jack looked at his Timex. "Only a few minutes more."

Hugh parted the drapes to view the embassy.

"Primakovski walks around the garden at precisely 1500 hours," said Jack, adopting spy craft speak. "I hope this Sudakov guy joins him."

"He will. Our team set up a drop for him in Moscow. He gave us two more canisters of microfiche with files we wanted and a note that he would join his boss in the garden at 3:00 p.m." Hugh mumbled about the stupidity of the Russians remaining at this location after the Sheraton was built. "It's not as if they're unaware the hotel overlooks the garden." Hugh's fingers toyed with the heavy drapes, slid them a bit wider, and opened the window. He and Jack had an unobstructed view. "Look; there they are."

Room 317 was a perfect location from which to hear almost everything the Russians were saying. Both Jack and Hugh knew that people who speak a second language fluently use the gestures—winks, nods, tongue clicks, and head bobs—of native speakers. Clearly, they were not speaking Arabic. Primakovski's hand jabbing and shoulder shrugging were strictly Russian.

When the two men completed their twice-around stroll, Primakovski went back into the embassy.

"We've heard enough and seen enough to know we're on track. I'm happy with what we've learned, and Pandora will be pleased too," Hugh said.

After the embassy door closed, Sudakov moved to the center of the garden and leaned on a eucalyptus tree near a centerpiece fountain and a flamboyant red-and-orange royal poinciana, deep in thought, twisting his wedding ring.

Hugh drew a breath, let go of the drape and turned to Jack. "He knows he's being watched. If he follows the plan, he will show up in the bar at the Semiramis Hotel with more information."

It's not a game anymore, Jack thought. *This is exciting. I'll get this guy to tell me exactly what the Russians are doing.* He set his jaw with determination.

Hugh put his hand on Jack's shoulder and waited for him to speak.

"The Semiramis."

"Exactly."

TWENTY-ONE

Semiramis Hotel

J ack's cab struggled through thick Cairo traffic to stop at an apartment building two blocks from the Semiramis Hotel. "Be cautious," Pandora had said. "If anyone follows you, it won't be locals; it will be Russians." He turned to look out the cab's back window. The number of people he felt were following him was expanding by the day.

He walked through the apartment lobby, out a back door, and down to a staircase leading to an alley. Boys kicking a soccer ball in the street ignored him when he stepped into a second apartment building and exited across from the Semiramis's kitchen door. Chefs banging pots and pans must have thought he was a new assistant manager when he passed through the kitchen, heading toward the semicircular lobby.

Marble-framed twenty-foot mirrors reflected beyond the hotel's pool a scene unchanged by the centuries. In the perfumed heat from a generous display of flowers, the Nile River shimmered in herringbone waves. Curving past the hotel's docks, becalmed sailboats drifted toward Alexandria like Moses's little reed boat.

Jack turned left into the lobby bar and approached a table near a swinging door that led to the card room. The bar was almost empty except for a couple of German businessmen talking too loudly at a cocktail table and an Englishman regaling the bartender with dirty jokes. Jack ordered a bitter lemon on ice and then took off his college ring and placed it on the table.

An unkempt bear of a man entered the bar and walked toward Jack, head down. The man made a clumsy show of sliding his wedding ring off, fumbling with it. He put it in his pocket and said, "I am Sudakov."

Jack chuckled. "I wouldn't have guessed."

Sudakov plopped into the brown padded armchair opposite Jack, shouting at the bartender. "Double vodka."

His unease probably stemmed from the risk of being seen in a bar with a non-Russian. He spoke first. "I may have been followed. Maybe I lost the guy. Anyway, I don't have much time."

Sudakov was about six two, with pudge-heavy features, a crowded face, thick eyebrows, and small hands. He would push the scale way past whatever number equaled obese. Jack waited, watching Sudakov shift in his chair.

Avoiding direct eye contact, speaking in guttural, rudimentary English, Sudakov said, "You are American spy? Have spy job in DC?"

"DC?"

The Russian smiled. "You see, I know America—maybe better than you."

"DC, where our capital is located? The District of Columbia?"

"Why you say Columbia? It is America district. Say District of America." Sudakov's thin-lipped grin edged toward playful.

Jack did not hide his irritation. "If you don't start talking, you may never see it."

"I report to Yevgeny Primakovski. He gets orders directly from Brezhnev. I know their thinking, their plans. I can tell what is going on—our involvement in Iran."

"That's good, Sudakov. We know Khomeini is colluding with Brezhnev, but we need proof. Also, the Slovetsky Park microfiche you gave us is not enough; it has limited information." Jack kept his voice moderate and pulled an envelope from his suit pocket. "So I've made a list of what has to be confirmed. I want backup for each one of these points, with detail."

Jack found his energy building. He was the front man, facing a guy who had probably aced KGB courses like How to Kill an American 101. Jack concentrated on his assignment, which was to bleed the Russian's secrets, use the information about the hostages, and eliminate the Russian if his markers were not met. Jack had never taken How to Kill a Russian 101; that would be a job for someone else.

"Stupid, stupid analysts you have ... stupid." Sudakov's temples flushed. "It had information you couldn't know. Your stupid analysts had secrets a week before it was in *Izvestia* newspaper. Microfiche said that famous agronomist will go Egypt, help increase crop growing. Plus Russia donate a billion for mechanical irrigation for project in desert. He is top KGB guy, here already."

"We already knew about Primakovski," said Jack without changing his expression.

"After debriefing with him I go to my new post in Kuwait and must prepare Gulf States report for Bahrain meeting. I think Primakovsi suspicious about me. If KGB think I plan to defect, they cut out my heart with old knife."

Sudakov's blue shirt was soaked with sweat. He gulped his vodka as though it were the last drink on Earth. The Russian was beginning to loosen up, stretching both arms along the top of the vinyl booth. His baritone exhalation began the story. "The Russians want Iran so we get route to warm-water port. Kremlin give Primakovski mandate to promote Russian interests in the whole Middle East. When I get to Kuwait, I will find out more about Russia plans. Americans want to know what Russia is doing in Tehran? I can tell you exactly."

The vodkas calmed Sudakov's nervousness, so Jack decided to ratchet up. "Okay, Big Bear, I can make sure you're extracted, but understand there are conditions. You will have to help me prove your value. Got it?"

The bear nodded, folded the "shopping list," and sat up straight, ready to leave.

"Tell us the timing and who the key Iranian people are. Get us solid information. If you do, it's USA. If you don't, enjoy Leningrad."

Jack walked a couple of blocks from the Semiramis and hailed a taxi to the Sheraton. Pandora was waiting, seated in a curved private alcove. Her slight hand wave motioned him to the single chair facing her, putting his back to the restaurant's lunch crowd, ignoring clandestine basics: never sit with your back to the door.

The section chief wore a multicolored tunic, fitting in with local fashion, presenting herself simply as another modestly dressed tourist. Pandora tugged the lightweight garment, draping it over her shoulders. "Well?" she asked without a hint of emotion.

Her tone was clear; MI6 people were interested in results and did not give a damn for him. He flipped a curt "Fine, thanks, how about you?"

"Hugh is on the way, Jack. Meanwhile, I want to know what you learned today."

"Sudakov met the description—as bulky as he appeared in the photos, his mannerisms slow, drudging, reflecting a guy who did not appear to have much interest in his job."

Pandora sat back in the banquette. "Continue."

"Okay, you know the man who was with him— Primakovski. Short, heavy, sixty or so, gray-and-black hair combed straight back, bushy black eyebrows; he was poking his finger in the air as he and Sudakov walked. They were speaking in Russian but switched to Arabic when two office workers came out of the embassy for a stroll. Hugh understood what they discussed, and I confirmed with Sudakov that he is taking up his post at their embassy in Kuwait. We only have a few days before he leaves."

"What else did you learn at the Semiramis?" Pandora asked.

Over a loudspeaker, a muezzin was calling every Muslim within earshot to afternoon prayer.

"Hi," Hugh said.

He walked up behind Jack's chair, breaking Jack's concentration on Pandora. That was a failure; Hugh could have been anyone.

"I'm just getting caught up with Jack," Pandora said.

Jack continued. "The most concerning thing is that Sudakov's boss may be suspicious. I gave him the questions you guys compiled, and I've set up another meeting with him for tomorrow. I want to keep this moving so I can get back to Tehran and Farideh."

Pandora sat up straight, her back rigid. "I understand, Jack, and now we need to talk with you about the photos taken in Khaki's office. Only two of the companies listed on the ledger pages were active in the business, and they were small-time gunrunners. The rest were straw companies. That's two hits in twelve pages."

"Those pictures were taken in a hurry."

Pandora nodded.

"We have another interesting picture, Jack," said Hugh. "It's of you. One of Furlong's locals took it."

"Of me? What do you mean of me?"

"You were getting into a car with the second-largest arms dealer in the world, Khaki's number one—Ali. It was in the parking lot at Mehrabad Airport."

Ten seconds of silence followed. "Okay, guess you think I'm too green at this stuff to understand what is going on, so … you tell me what's going on."

Pandora explained. "Jack, you have to be very careful of that man. He would kill you in an instant. Among all the Turks living in Iran, he is the most feared. We know the Russians are getting tough with Iran, pushing their own agenda. Since the turncoat Russian is being transferred to Kuwait, you are to go back there too and finish picking him dry."

TWENTY-TWO

Revelations

Returning to the Semiramis for their second meeting, Jack placed two glasses on a table in a recessed corner of the bar.

Screwing up the Russian reputation for always being late, Sudakov was on time. He gulped his vodka, put down the glass, picked up Jack's and smelled it. "Water?" He sniffed the glass a second time. "Why you not drink with me, Mr. Devlin?"

"Look, Sudakov; I'm here to do business. Buy me a drink in New York."

"Another vodka," Sudakov shouted to the bartender.

Jack had to move fast, before Sudakov's drinking took him down the path of a babbling drunk. "Look, your value to the US is to tell us the specifics of why the Russians are kissing up to Iran. I want hard facts—no bullshit. Do you have answers from the list I gave you?"

Sudakov's face reddened. "You'll get it. I need time."

Jack adjusted his approach. He smiled and became the good guy. "Look, Vladimir; I know life has not been easy for you. You haven't been appreciated. Our guys in Washington told me your dad died in the gulags even after all he did for Stalin. Had to be shitty for you, losing your dad that way. Stalin was a monster. You won't find people like that in America."

Sudakov's sagging jowls and the puffy bags under bloodshot eyes gave him the hung-down look of a bloodhound.

"Hard to get such information, you know."

"Yeah, but you can do it, Vlad. You're good. Washington thinks you're really good. They can't wait to welcome you, introduce you to some congressmen and sexy American girls, and give you a medal. I can put in a good word for you—get you into a protection program in California."

Sudakov lost the generic KGB expressionless face, beaming at his new American friend. "In my country everything is sick, ugly; but there is one thing you can count on, one thing you can trust. It is vodka. You can always trust vodka; it is friend. It is not problem; it is answer. I love America. *Za Zdarovje.*"

"You'll have all the vodka you can drink in America, as long as you can get this to me. Do it quick, or I'll send a case of Tennessee bourbon to Primakovski with your compliments."

The brief Jack read at the British embassy had spelled it out. Sudakov had several reasons to want a geographical and political restart. He was overwhelmed with debt, his wife wanted a divorce, and booze had compromised him enough to earn a formal reprimand from the Committee for State Security of the USSR. His career was falling apart, and he knew it. His next post would be a freezing, stinking, windowless gulag in Siberia or a view of Times Square from an expensive hotel room.

Sudakov mumbled, "Da. Give me more vodka. I tell you more."

Jack held the glass for a few seconds. "A film will probably be made of your heroic defection, your allegiance to America. Women will fight to be on your arm; mothers will point to you, telling their children America will be safe because of you and your gift to America."

"Okay, Primakovski's plan for Iran is to move hostages to Azerbaijan border, maybe get Azerbaijanis to kill all." Sudakov loosened his tie. "Here is news for you: Ayatollah Khomeini plans to bring Islamist revolution all over Middle East. USSR will be secret partner."

Jack fumed. The thought of the hostage crisis triggering a Middle East revolution was not new; the *New York Times* wrote about it. But Russian support in the growth of the Islamic Revolution was new. Sudakov did not understand the impact of the problems that would follow if anything happened to the American hostages. Extreme Islamic radicals would become terrorists, and the torch to light their fire would be American retaliation to such an atrocity.

The Russian continued. "Okay, I tell you tomorrow when hostages be moved. Then Americans need act fast; get them out or they die. I on your side now, Jack. You need me."

"I'll advise that you are cooperating." Jack thumped his index finger on Sudakov's chest. "Get the details. I'm leaving now. You get ready for our next meeting."

The KGB spy slunk back in his chair and grunted, "Bartender, bring vodka—double."

Jack left the Russian to wallow in the stateless realities of a defector. Turncoats cannot trust people; their betrayal turns inward and self-doubt rises. They are the essence of hypocrisy. Before his KGB bosses would find out about his treachery, Sudakov would realize that the integrity he had lost would never be regained.

Langley's analysis was that nationalistic persecution had not motivated Sudakov to cross the line. Like other turncoats, he had been sucked into the allure of the America highlighted in movies shown at secret Komsomol parties— underground movies with John Wayne on a horse, Ringling Brothers elephants parading down a main street in Iowa, and *West Side Story*, a favorite. The movies would have watered the seeds of longing for freedom, sprouting them in any Russian's soul.

The Russian caught his image in a mirror. He was beaming, thinking about his new life.

When the waiter returned with another vodka, he asked, "Everything all right, sir?" as the Russian grabbed the drink off the tray.

Without removing his eyes from the glass, Sudakov responded, "Fine, my friend. Everything fine." Sudakov held the glass up to the light, squinted through the clear alcohol, tossed it down, and handed it to the waiter. He struggled to his feet.

"Before you go sir … the bill."

"What? The American was supposed to pay. I didn't bring any money."

"Quite all right, sir; I'll send the boy to the embassy with you to get the money. The Russian one, right, sir?"

Jack jumped out of the cab, rushed into the Sheraton past crowds waiting for the elevator, and hurried up the stairs to debrief Hugh about his meeting with Sudakov. The door of room 317 cracked open before Jack slid his skeleton key into the lock.

Hugh grabbed Jack's arm to pull him in. "We have company," he said.

Pandora stood at the window, her hand holding back the drape. Jack dropped his jacket on the foot of the disheveled bed and grinned. He turned toward Hugh, still standing by the door. "Nice nap?"

"Shove it," replied Hugh.

Pandora moved to the couch, smoothed her dress and sat down. Hugh joined her and said, "Okay, Jack, what's new?"

Reaching for a cloth to wipe sweat from his forehead, Jack said, "When Sudakov gets to his new post in Kuwait, his first assignment is to organize a meeting. Primakovski is summoning all the men in his command to a meeting at the Russian embassy in Bahrain next week."

"Go on," said Pandora.

"The Russians are using the animosity between America and Iran as leverage. I told Sudakov if the hostages were disbursed, he would be of no further use."

"You seem to have taken this into your own hands, Mr. Devlin," said Pandora.

"It was in his hands all along," said Hugh, smiling.

"Sudakov agreed to meet me in Kuwait with a copy of the Russian strategy for Iran. Once validated, he will have earned his ticket to the United States and we will have to take him in. Agreed?" Jack moved to a small marble table by the couch, grabbed an Évian and waited.

Pandora was pensive, her eyes cast down. She lifted her head, gave a simple nod, and said, "Agreed."

Jack walked to the window and slid the drape to take another look at the Russian embassy.

"Once you get to Kuwait, you'll be walking a tightrope. If this goes bonkers, or if Sudakov's playing us and his actual assignment is to nab a CIA agent to cart off to Moscow for interrogation, you might be that target. They'll get away with it, too, because the US will deny you exist," said Hugh.

"As will MI6," Pandora added.

"You've got solid potential for a long career, Jack," said Hugh, "'cause I'll recommend you for a permanent position. But you gotta complete the assignment—get that ledger. Stripping Sudakov is great; the ledger is worth much more. Don't forget that's your primary responsibility."

"Don't you forget, Hugh, my primary responsibility is to get my girlfriend safely out of Iran." Jack took on an expression he had learned in spy school—no expression. He felt gnawing irritation that Hugh thought more about the ledger than the intel he was getting from Sudakov. With a nod to Pandora, he said, "Forget about this becoming my career; it's hard to believe I've let myself get in this deep. The only thing making sense out of this is to get the hostages out and home safe in the US."

"And Farideh?" interrupted Pandora.

"You got it. Her sister too … and getting their father buried in a tomb forever."

"What are your plans?" asked Pandora.

"Now that you have added this assignment, I'll have to make some adjustments and keep my meeting with Sudakov in Kuwait. But I want your word that the commitment to extricate him is solid. I want to know how it will happen, where, and when." Jack felt a rush of adrenaline surge through his body when he realized he was telling two senior-level spies what he wanted and they were agreeing. "I'll be in Kuwait by lunch tomorrow. Who do I contact?"

Hugh answered, "In baggage claim at the Kuwait airport, you'll see a woman holding a small package with a red ribbon. Ask if she got the gift in the souk. Her response will be, 'Yes, Baba Souk.'"

"A woman carrying a present? Hardly needs a coded check-in."

"The code qualifies you. I met the lady once at Langley. Nice figure—can't be hidden by a chador." Hugh winked, avoiding Pandora's combative stare.

Jack stuffed his Dopp kit and a couple of shirts into his bag. He paused at the door. "I'll hang out the Do Not Disturb sign."

TWENTY-THREE

Ordered to Kuwait

I n the baggage claim, Jack spotted his target and imagined everyone else did too. A black hijab covered her head, honoring local tradition, but did not hide her attractiveness. Silky black hair poked out beneath a head-to-toe chador that almost concealed her dark eyes. He nodded toward the brightly wrapped gift. "Got that for me in the souk?"

"Yes, the Baba Souk," she said in Singapore-accented English.

He followed her to a monstrous thug holding the door of a midnight-black Range Rover. Jack jumped in behind a window separating the brute from the rear compartment.

The exquisite Asian lady placed the package between them, lit a cigarette, and introduced herself. "I am Kyi."

"Singapore?"

"No, close. My accent is Burmese. My mother married a British colonel in Rangoon."

"Tatakallam 'arabīyah?" Jack asked.

"Sure, I speak Arabic, like the driver, so let's stick with the Queen's English."

She held a finger to her lips. "I'm a field liaison specialist, Gulf States."

MI6 was introducing him to the kind of ladies he used to try to find himself, and they were doing just fine. Working with a petite, lithe, tan-skinned woman with large black eyes confirmed what he learned in London: Spies don't look like spies.

"Let's talk, Kyi; bring me up to date. What's going on with the Russian?"

"He's here. Reported to his embassy yesterday. He will be extracted by the Americans in a few days."

"Whoa, wait a minute." Jack turned his shoulder to block the rearview mirror and inquisitive glances from the driver. "Sudakov is not leaving Kuwait until I get more information. Who set the timetable—the Brits or the Americans?"

"The CIA. They're handling this one. They did say you'll make the specific decisions of when and where. The Americans want to get the Russian in their hands as soon as possible, get him to Ramstein, Germany, for debriefing, where they can be more thorough. It was their agent, Ebanks, who told London you have Sudakov's trust and you're in charge. Something about the Russian being just a part of a much bigger assignment you and he are working on in Iran."

Jack nodded.

"When you're ready, give us the time and location where a team will pick him up and take him to the airport. But, Jack, if something triggers an earlier extraction, he will see this teddy bear," she said, unwrapping the package. "It will be on the rear shelf of a black Chevy parked in the Fourth Ring Road circle. The Russian drives through the circle twice a day from the housing compound to work. Tell him to look for the teddy bear. If he spots it, he has been discovered. He is to continue around the circle and take the airport exit. Both our agencies have signed off on this."

"A teddy bear? Who came up with the teddy bear idea?"

"I did," she said, squaring off to get eye-to-eye contact.

"Right, good idea, Kyi. Real sharp espionage stuff."

His sarcasm was ignored.

Now Jack would have to pull more Mid East detail from Sudakov fast. When he got to Ramstein, the guys would get his complete life story. They could extract a confession from a corpse. If the KGB operative did not enjoy talking, there would be a seat waiting on a high-altitude jet that would eject him over East Berlin in a parachute with an American flag. If he decided not to pull the pin to activate the parachute, that would be his choice.

"Higher-ups can't accept that a lone agent could strip a defector; they'll want to do it with a committee at Ramstein." Faint beads of perspiration dotted her forehead. "Head office mandarins always think they can do our job better."

He nodded in agreement. "When I have a come-to-Jesus meeting with the Russian, I'll get what I want from him, and it won't take more than a couple of days."

Kyi stubbed out her cigarette and gazed at Jack under thin raised eyebrows. "We got a telex you wanted to speak to one of our doctors on a personal matter. Reggie Smyth is our house consultant—takes care of burns, breaks, but not boobs. Have to go back to the UK for that." She laughed.

"Looks like you've already made that trip. Nice work," Jack said.

Kyi scowled and pushed back to sit up straight against the uncomfortable seat.

"I'm sure Dr. Smyth will be fine; I just need to ask a medical question."

Kyi checked her watch. "Well, Reg is on the way to your hotel, and here we are." The Rover stopped on the less-crowded side street next to Le Méridien.

Kyi chuckled as Jack crawled over her to get out and said, "The doc will be able to help get you fixed up straight as a ramrod. Don't worry, though; happens to a lot of guys."

Within ten minutes, Jack was in his usual room, checking it out in a routine MI6 would have admired; but the sweep was interrupted by a knock. "Who is it?"

"Reggie Smyth here."

The small, bespectacled Smyth must have had to use all his strength when knocking. He was too small to be called a lightweight. Jack motioned the man in, glanced up and down the hallway, and pulled the door closed. Smyth's handshake was sweaty and limp, the handle of his doctor's bag soaked.

"The ambassador's office asked me to pop in. Said you had a personal problem to discuss—only kind I handle, the personal ones. Those community diseases are best left to the National Health lads." In soft, singsong prose that identified him as Welsh, he carried on. He shook his long black hair like an afghan hound in from the rain. "Sit over here?" he asked, pointing to the only chair in the room.

Jack nodded.

The stuffy Englishman placed his bag on the floor and said, "I've brought the forms for you to fill out after I examine you. Must have the papers in order. Tell me your symptoms."

Jack shook his head, amused that British bureaucracy had turned a simple, straightforward request into a foreign expedition.

"Look, Dr. Smyth, no paperwork. It is personal but not related to me or my business. A family member is not well, and I need to learn all I can about her problem."

"Okay, chap, get on with it. What's the matter?" The doctor's eye had a gleam, as if hoping to hear some lurid, oozing description of a terminal problem.

"The lady has some kind of rare kidney disease and is hooked up to a machine for dialysis. Her sister is afraid she'll die unless she gets proper treatment continuously."

"Do you want me to see her?"

"It would help. Could you make a house call in Iran?" Jack teased.

"I'm afraid I can't be much help, Mr. Devlin. The British mission there is closed." He reached for his bag.

"No, Dr. Smyth, I'm really not asking you to go to Iran. I want to know what happens if the dialysis machine fails and she can't get another."

"If the machine fails, she could get uremic poisoning, or her potassium levels might increase, which could bring on cardiac arrest."

"How long can she live if the machine stops working?"

"Depends, chap. She could survive one or two weeks. But a slow end—usually painful. Progressive multiorgan failure is not nice."

"Can she travel?"

"Yes, but she shouldn't go more than four days without dialysis or complications will begin. Anything else, chappy?"

"No, and I trust you'll keep this matter confidential?" Jack locked his eyes onto Dr. Smyth as if binding him to secrecy.

Smyth extended his limp, perspiring hand and left.

Jack latched the door, caught his reflection from the bathroom mirror, and was appalled at his weary, almost gaunt appearance. The weight of Smyth's comments wore heavy—heavier than the wet gulf air stifling the room. If Leah was going to survive, he would have to get her out of Iran—carefully.

TWENTY-FOUR

An Omani Dhow

The ancient Middle East had always held a fascination for Jack, but never more than on this April morning while watching the crowd waiting to board an Omani dhow—a ferry from Kuwait to Bahrain. "High value" ticket holders had boarded. Jack was irritated that he had a "regular" ticket and upset that Sudakov had insisted their next meeting would be on a dhow. Time lost on the two-and-a-half-hour trip to Manama was a waste. The evening flight back would take only fifty minutes, and there was only one flight a day.

It was Thursday, the beginning of the Arab weekend. The days were hot at dawn, blistering by ten, and then unbearable. And not a little unbearable—*impossibly* unbearable. The few Bedouins in the raucous crowd appeared to be impervious to heat. They wore sandal-length white cotton robes, their heads covered with white-and-red-checkered keffiyehs falling in a flair, shielding their necks. Bedouins believed wearing robes had a cooling effect that protected them from the heat and blowing desert sands. The Arab mind confounded reality.

The crowd shuffled in a jagged throng, anxious to funnel through a gate and board the ancient wooden ark bobbing against a crumbling fish pier. More a gang than a crowd, the weaving humanity shouted, pushed, elbowed, and fought for a better position to board. Jack watched shoeless Pakistanis in striped skirts stand apart from East Indian laborers in mismatched multicolored shirts and blouson jackets. Men kept worldly possessions in gunnysacks slung over their shoulders or bundled under their arms. A few Caucasian business types, sweating in open-neck shirts, did their best to avoid close contact with the smelly, salt-sweating crowd. In the packs jostling to get to the front of the line, languages and dialects clashed in curses and shouts at guards barring the narrow gate to the creaking dhow.

The riff-raff's shouts subsided to a cheer when the guards ripped the chains off the gates. In the rabid crush rushing aboard, brown-robed Yeminis, curved daggers sheathed in their blue midriff sashes, swished through the Pakistanis for seats on the rail. Indians and Bangladeshis gathered in a knot at the bow. Qat ballooned the cheeks of four Yeminis glaring at the South Asians.

Jack let the crowd move aboard while he watched for two MI6 special agents from Karachi. Kyi had told him they would be aboard for his protection. "They will blend in," she had said. "You won't, so don't bother looking for them."

Dante must have sent the old dhow from hell, Jack thought as the ship readied to leave the dock. Beyond the harbor entrance, rollicking green waves waited to rock and roll the dhow's passengers across her slotted decks. The pungent stink of seasick, unwashed humans would soon overcome odors of fish rotting in the holds under serrated deck planks.

Omani crewmen in skirts drooping to the tops of their calves wore shiny sleeveless vests that exposed their brown torsos—glossy with sweat. Two Omanis pulled lines off the dock; the third tended a tiller on a raised storm deck. Jack leaned on the aft-deck rail behind the helmsman under the arc of the whip the helmsman whirled to keep passengers out of his way. The dhow cleared the harbor, tacking through bobbing water taxis, fishing boats, and a Kuwaiti police launch. The shadow of a slow-moving German-flagged cargo ship momentarily blocked the searing sun.

Ten minutes after castoff, Sudakov emerged from the mob, walking toward the stern, pushing through crouching passengers, his pudgy fingers clothespinning his nose. With his authoritative voice booming, "Get out of the way!" in flawless Arabic, he scattered passengers on their annual journey to homes in South Asia and Pakistan.

Russian spies look like spies, except in the case of Vladimir Sudakov. He looked like an oversize Russian oaf who couldn't spy on schoolgirls. Thirty pounds overweight, perspiration saturated his white wash-and-wear shirt. His thick, heavy-soled government-issued shoes were at least size 13 plus. Sudakov looked more like a big farm boy lumbering toward him than a KGB spy. He would stand out in any crowd.

The old wooden dhow creaked and shuddered, sailing into the main shipping channel.

Sudakov perched on a coil of heavy hemp rope, holding a newspaper. His watery red eyes swam above black-and-blue bags, strained by hangovers and too many cheroots. "My stupid embassy too cheap to buy plane ticket to Bahrain. Sorry, but listen, please. Iran now want to end hostage crisis. Russia says no, thinks Iran should keep upper hand for bargaining with Americans. Russia believe America has plan to rescue your people. You know about it, yes?"

"Of course," Jack said, although he did not know anything about a rescue operation, even though it made sense.

"I have meeting at Bahrain embassy. I get details when Iran will move. You tell your guys, get me out. It will not take long for KGB to discover I double agent." Looking like the most terrified KGB operative on the planet, Sudakov continued with scared-to-death intensity. "Today I find out if transfer to Kuwait is permanent or being sent back to Russia for review. Jack, you'll get me out, right?"

Jack shielded his mouth to avoid his lips being read. "You'll be extracted as soon as you give details of the move. In the meantime, you need to act routine with your assignments. Don't get sent to Tehran, or you're sunk. We will not be able to get you out of Iran."

Sudakov reached out a hand to steady himself as the dhow turned into the wind. He passed his folded *International Herald Tribune* to Jack. "Has microfiche, sports section. Me, I don't like sports."

Sudakov, for all his faults, had an innocence and a childlike manner. "If you think you've been discovered or run into any problems, call this number from a pay phone and follow the steps listed," Jack said, handing him a slip of paper. "Extraction is based on your habits, so listen carefully. On your way to work, you turn into the circle of the Fourth Ring Road. Keep your eyes open for an American car parked on the side of the road. There will be a teddy bear in the car's back window. When you see it, do not go to your embassy; take the exit for the airport. Our guys will make contact with you on the airport road; you'll be in Germany by dark."

"Teddy bear is stupid idea. Stupid plan. You just want information. You got everything, and I am dead man tortured to death on the floor of Lubyanka."

Jack's growing confidence emerged in a smile. "If your info is good, you'll be saved by a stuffed teddy bear. If not? You'll be the one stuffed."

Jack moved in to hammer his point. The fish rotting below the deck smelled better than Sudakov's breath. "Remember: we also want to know details of Russia's plans for Egypt and Kuwait and what they plan for Ayatollah Khomeini. Make sure what you get at your embassy today has the depth we need, and you'll get what you want." Jack palmed his fist. "If later on we find out it is not valid, I will nail you to a Russian cross on the roof of the tallest building in Times Square." Sudakov's breath won; Jack pulled back, his adrenaline pumping.

Sudakov grumbled agreement in the resonant baritone of a Russian Orthodox priest.

Jack's assignment with the KGB agent was close to ending. He was satisfied that his work was on schedule and the intel would soon be in Washington. A few more pieces needed to fall, and the KGB would be missing their key Arabic-speaking spy and the US could be finalizing a rescue plan for the hostages.

TWENTY-FIVE

The Noose Tightened

"**Y**ou tea drinkers make horrible coffee," Jack commented to the cockney chef while waiting for Pandora Quince. The staff dining room at the British embassy in Kuwait still smelled like breakfast.

Jack looked at Pandora admiringly, but he held no stronger emotions. Her skill in running MI6 operations in the Middle East had earned the support of her boss, Algernon Trivelpiece, and the head of CIA operations in Europe and the Middle East, Hugh Ebanks. She and nearly everyone else he had met seemed solid, but the CIA and MI6 were all about duplicity. Jack wondered if operatives like Hugh carried that duplicity into personal relationships.

"Hello, Jack." Pandora nodded as she slid into a chair. "Hugh is right behind me."

A hot desert wind rattled through the room when Hugh opened the door. "Good news, Jack. Did you tell him, Pandora?"

"Not yet."

Hugh's chair scraped the sticky linoleum as he dragged it to sit next to Pandora. "Okay, listen up. Langley further verified that Sudakov's sources would have participated in plans the USSR had for Iran. The files you got from Sudakov were solid, and there was a hidden benefit. Langley found a coded message to a mole who had wormed his way into CIA operations. He was arrested yesterday, so they want us to move this deal faster. But first, congrats to you on your work with the Russian." Hugh shook his hand in a viselike grip. "Second, Langley cautions that the mole may know about you, so get the job done and watch your ass."

"Watch yours, Hugh. I'm not worried."

Jack caught Pandora's smile as he headed to the coffeepot. "The timing to get Sudakov out should be moved up," he said. "We can't wait for Langley to deep-dive the mole for every scrap of information he has."

Hugh responded, "It will be tomorrow. Langley believes his cover has been blown. So let's get him the hell out of here. The car will be dropped off in the roundabout by one of our best agents, Billy Holiday. He will put the teddy bear in its back window at dawn."

Jack laughed. "You know, no one would believe this stuff. I thought you guys were sophisticated."

"Sophisticated people get killed. We get the job done. Get Sudakov out of here, and then get back to your primary mission. Remember the reason I brought you into this deal, Jack. No one but you can get to Khaki, and no one but me can get your Farideh out."

"Got it, Hugh. Relax. You're getting worked up. Sounds like the ledger is more important than Farideh or me."

"Don't kid yourself, Jack. This is not about your love life; it's about business and keeping promises. Anyway, who cares if people think we're sophisticated? The American government is full of nitpickers and bureaucrats, and I hate them—well, some of them. Don't forget I'm just an immigrant from a Caribbean island and I'll never get higher in the CIA 'cause I'm black, and

Pandora will never get higher at MI6 'cause she's a woman. We'd probably both be better off if we worked for the KGB."

"Stop it, Hugh, enough," Pandora said.

Hugh began to pace, head down, muttering. "Sorry, let's go over this. When Sudakov heads toward the airport, agents will follow. Two other guys will be on the plane to Frankfurt. He won't know they're there unless something goes wrong. That guy has been good for us. We got more than expected, like the info that the Revolutionary Guard will start moving the hostages by the end of this month."

Pandora's long taupe skirt swished when she stood. Tilting her head toward the kitchen, she yelled, "More tea, vicar," to an unholy cook who responded quickly with a steaming kettle. "Both of us are pleased, Jack; you are almost finished with this part of the job. We will arrange a special envelope for you. Dinar, pounds, dollars? I suggest sterling."

"What do you mean 'almost finished'?"

"Well, you have to get back into Iran. Furlong's people are the only two locals left in Tehran. They're putting together a plan to cover you because Khaki's unpredictable," Pandora said. She sat back, crossed her legs, and added, "Now, there are a few changes to make. Then it's all hands on deck for the job in Iran."

"What changes?"

"Nothing for you to worry about," she said.

Jack felt a noose tightening. He got up and walked across the room, looked back at the two agents, and felt trusted, valued, but wondered if his trust of Hugh and Pandora had been misplaced. They were intelligence agents whose world was covered by a blanket that shut out the lights of reality. They could peer out, but no one could peer in. Spies can see in the dark; it is their way of life. It was seeping into his blood.

TWENTY-SIX

Vladimir and Natasha

O n the outskirts of the city, near the Fourth Ring Road, a handful of Eastern European diplomatic posts kept ugly apartment buildings for staff. The Russian presence was the largest; Sudakov's apartment, one of the smallest. Every day, his wife reminded him she used to live in better quarters.

The Russian-style block had one building housing nonessential staff on the first two floors, married couples on levels three and four, and screaming children running up and down all four floors. The Sudakovs were on a two-year wait list for an adjoining building that housed officer-rank staff. Sudakov felt that only Soviets could design and build such a rotten and unattractive compound. Behind the towering state security walls, the enigmatic monstrosity came straight out of Leningrad. Stinking smells of cabbage and boiling beets seeped from every door—even closed ones. An undercover KGB agent working as a clerk at the Russian embassy would live like a clerk.

Sudakov lumbered up the four floors to his flat, hating every step. He opened the door, hoping no one would be home, shouting, "I'm here."

On a tiny counter, a small steel-blade fan whirred next to a yellow plastic tub piled high with dirty dishes and a sink full of pots and rags. On a red-stained plastic carving board, grated beets, a cup of sugar, an onion, and strong Russian vinegar were ready for the beaten-up pot that was also used for washing underwear. Little Natalia sat in a bouncy chair, licking the rim of the vinegar cap.

Sudakov had seen pictures of Russian heroes fixed to colorless kitchen and bedroom walls in other apartments. But not his. Their flat featured a smiling Stalin standing next to Natasha's father, General Anastas Lavarenkov. Another photo, torn and wrinkled, showed Natasha's father playing cards with Stalin. When he thought back to the night he crumpled that picture, it brought a warm feeling to his large belly. Since the long battles with Germany at St. Petersburg, through every Kremlin war and putsch, Natasha Sudakov's father had survived. He won every fight, enjoyed an unbroken stream of victories in politics, and rose to become a general in the military. His forty-six-inch chest was not broad enough to wear all the medals he'd earned. General Lavarenkov was the model Russian hero until he met an enemy he could not defeat. His only child, his headstrong daughter, Natasha, had fallen in love and married an imbecilic KGB officer—Vladimir Sudakov.

The old warrior had warned his daughter she would come to regret having met Sudakov in the Komsomol. He could have been talking to a deaf person. Natasha Lavarenkov believed her father would come around, that he would come to love and respect her Vladimir, and that their children would bring him joy in his old age. She was wrong. Her father had proven his wisdom over time.

Central Supply, a machination of the Soviet Army, provided furnishings for each apartment, including an oversize picture of Prime Minister Leonid Brezhnev, his suit heavy with medals. Brezhnev's picture hung over their bed, next to the bigger one of Stalin. A small pine table, two chairs, and a three-drawer bureau, too big for the cramped bedroom, filled the kitchen. The only window faced the Kuwait Desert. A single fan helped little, except to be the musical conductor for the syncopation of colorful metal beads draping the opening to the bedroom.

"You're here? I should care," said Natasha, looking up from her overstuffed chair, scowling at Sudakov. The massive woman struggled to get up, her usual anger intensified with spit and venom. "Vladimir Sudakov, you are a worthless oaf. Think I am stupid? You are the stupid—a coward. You think I don't know you love America more than Soviet Union? You snore and grunt and fart in your sleep, and you say stupid things. Who is Jack? Comrade Isvenko, next door, said no Jack at embassy; he checked."

The five hundred pounds of smelly, screaming toe-to-toe Russians were not engaged in lovemaking. She raved on; her comments stung her terrified husband. *She couldn't know,* he told himself, *but she told someone.* He had let something slip. His self-doubt was justified.

"If you even know someone with a stupid name of Jack, my father would call it treason. Go to your American friends, you imbecile. You are not good enough to be a Russian."

"Stop shouting!" Sudakov shouted within walls as thin as Ukrainian flatbread. Neighbors on every floor were quite used to shouting, fights, wailing wives, sexual exhortations, and crying children. No one would notice one more fight— except, perhaps, Comrade Isvenko.

Natasha would not stop. Standing stomach-to-stomach with Sudakov, she had his full attention. "Tomorrow I go to embassy and tell them me and Natalia want go home." She poked her husband in the chest right under the heart—a favorite spot. "My father will welcome me. He will take care of me—you don't. I hate you. Get out." Tears washed over the baby-bottom curves of her pimply red cheeks. Grabbing Natalia, she hip-separated the beads and lunged into the bedroom, ranting in street Russian.

Little Natalia, crying, reached out for her father, shouting, "Papa!"

He ignored her.

He was compromised. Even if Isvenko did not check the embassy, Moscow did not tolerate officers who would not keep family life out of their important jobs. USSR first, family second—this was the eternal Russian way. Unnerved, Sudakov noisily left the apartment, slamming the door, shaking the single-ply walls.

Taking the stairs two steps at a time, then three, then flying onto the landing, he ran for the parking lot. The government-issued Lada ground into gear. His sweaty palms clamped onto the car's little steering wheel as he turned left, heading for the phone booth in a petrol station a kilometer away. In an emergency, he was to dial the phone code Jack had supplied. One ring, hang up, dial again. One ring, hang up. Thirty minutes after the second call, he was to go to the seaside upper corner of the parking lot at the Kuwait Hilton. A contact would be waiting next to the pool. Sudakov made both calls.

The Lada exited the petrol station, chugging toward town. Sudakov tried to keep his mind quiet but found it impossible. In twenty-four hours, he would either be rescued by the Americans or handcuffed to mindless security apparatchiks on the way to the leaky, freezing dungeons below the River Neva.

Sudakov slipped the Lada into a narrow slot and walked toward the hotel. On his right, tables and chairs were set under regal palms, their low fronds swaying in the hot evening breeze. Near the steps to the pool, a portly balding man sat at a table edging the path. Cigar smoke curled around the *International Herald Tribune*, a newspaper Sudakov used to read from his days in the translator unit.

As Sudakov approached, the man stretched a cowboy boot, catching the bottom rung of a chair, turning it to block the Russian. Sudakov dropped into the seat, staring at the unsmiling man whose cowboy hat covered half the table. Whatever tradecraft Sudakov had learned, it had not prepared him for a fat American cowboy in a garden in Kuwait. Jack had never said anything about a cowboy.

"Who you?" asked Sudakov.

"Me, Bub? Just a friend of Jack's. You doin' okay, buddy boy?"

The Russian looked around, saw no one, and let loose his erupting frustration, brimming with red-hot steam about his marriage. "My wife has face of a pig. Her huge nose points up. Two big holes face me from her fat face every day. Her mouth is biggest hole; every word is a shout. She weigh twenty kilos more than me. She is pig."

The cowboy held up the palm of his hand. It was useless.

His arms flailing, Sudakov folded a fist, one finger jabbing in the air. "I hate her. She make our daughter with same pig nose, but I get even."

The cowboy waved both palms, trying again to silence Sudakov's rants.

"I go to America without them. You people get me out of here, fast." Breathless, he sputtered, "My pig wife suspicious. Told some guy from my embassy that I know American called Jack. Telling my boss tomorrow."

"Whoa, pony. Relax. You have problems with your wife? I have problems, you have problems—*oy vey*, we all have problems. I ordered drinks. Relax; here comes the waiter."

A sweating Bangladeshi brought two half-full glasses of ice and orange juice. The cowboy took a flask out of his boot and filled both glasses. Sudakov's was emptied before the flask got back to the boot. "How about another?" he asked. "What is it?"

"Bourbon, son. Good Kentucky bourbon."

"She is shitty pig. I tell you, she go to embassy, get plans for leave to Moscow." The Russian adjusted his chair, fixed his eyes on the cowboy, and said, "She call big shot father. He hate me too."

"Look at me, Russian. Look at me; watch my lips." Their heads nearly touched. "You calm down *now*. You have been trained to act calm; you must tough it out."

"Who are you anyway?" Sudakov asked.

"Call me Okie—the Okie from Muskogee. But you probably can't pronounce that." He stifled a belly laugh. "Look, kid, I don't know nothin' about you and don't want to. I'm a friend of Jack's, an accountant at our embassy, and he asked me to meet you. Shit, I'm no spy guy; I couldn't find my ass in the dark. I'm here to give you a message."

"Okay, but first need another bourbon."

The ham-fisted Okie grabbed his flask, poured two large shots, and looked over both his shoulders, a huge smile crossing his face. "That's how spies look around, right kid? Ha ha."

The laugh did not ease Sudakov's nerves. "What am I supposed to do?"

"Devlin says you're covered. He has a team watching you right now." He nodded toward a bronze Chevy in the parking lot where two men were fiddling with something under the hood. The Okie feigned a wave. "That team will be around until you leave. Jack is speeding things up, but it ain't easy to get Langley bureaucrat bullshitters to react. So here's what he wants you to do."

Sudakov tensed, apprehensive there would be more delay.

"Devlin says you are to go home, calm things down, and make your wife happy tonight. Get her to think it over. Apologize for being a jerk; admit you are one." The cowboy raised his glass in a mock toast. "See the bag there?" The Okie pointed to the base of the palm tree next to the table. "It's got chocolates and Russian candy in it. Jack expected you would screw it up, so use this stuff as a peace offering. Give Miss Piggy all she wants. Make her happy. You go home and stall her, because Jack needs a little more time. Now, I'm gone, sonny," he said, standing up. "This is my first and last spy trick; call me a one-trick pony. Don't screw up anymore, my friend. Hear me now?"

"You are funny man," said Sudakov.

"Maybe, kid, maybe, but what I know sure as shootin' is Jack says he got your teddy bear. Don't know what that's all about; you must be some kind of wimp. But I'm pretty sure that if you don't put out this fire with your wife, you ain't gettin' it back and you'll be tradin' it for a different bear—a Russian one. Good luck, Alice."

TWENTY-SEVEN

The Spy and the Teddy Bear

Three roads splayed from the round circle of the Fourth Ring Road. Commuters parked in the circle to wait for a rattletrap bus. One road led east to the city of Kuwait and Sudakov's embassy, another toward Saudi Arabia and the wastes of the Arabian Desert. The third was a clear shot to the airport. Two other exits were sand tracks—an urban planner's dream for future development. The broad circle encroached on the shrinking desert as Kuwait City spread out of its Middle Ages confines, forcing Bedouins toward the border with Iraq.

Every morning at eight o'clock, Sudakov said good-bye to Natasha, hoping it would be the last time, praying to see the teddy bear. Sudakov allowed only a half an hour to get to work; he was punctually late. It took forty-five minutes. Behind the wheel of his small, dark Lada, Vladimir Sudakov would enter the circle from the northwest on Al-Haub Road and take the exit for the city. For days his drive led to unsettling doubts that he would ever escape.

Sudakov replayed in his mind the instructions Jack had given him: Teddy bear, back deck window, black Chevy. If he spotted the bear, he had to drive normally—react as if he were heading to the airport, catching a flight. A white delivery truck would be tucked into palm groves precisely

2.4 kilometers from the Fourth Ring Road. The delivery truck driver would lead him deeper into the grove, where the creaking old Lada would be abandoned, the first leg of his relocation to America.

If the signal was in place and Sudakov missed it, he would continue his routine drive to the embassy and never be seen again. His next stop would be the notorious prison Lubyanka, for a session with a man called the Fish Scaler.

An iceberg could not cool Sudakov. The Lada, which lacked air conditioning, had no chance of taming the Kuwait heat and humidity. Yesterday morning had passed with no sign, no teddy bear, no extraction. His demons of doubt proclaimed that the Americans had suckered him dry, that they did not need him anymore. Now his rotten wife had guessed why he could not sleep. His plump, sweaty hands felt as if they could melt the metal steering wheel.

Special Agent Billy Holiday entered the traffic circle of the Fourth Ring Road. His assignment was specific and uncomplicated even though a life depended on getting it right. In the early-morning rush, no one would notice if he drove around the circle a couple of times before choosing a place to park his black Chevy. He would have to accomplish his task before the Russian's Lada entered the roundabout. An early-morning wind whipped little dancing dust devils of desert sand a foot high and then plopped them into a whisper of dust when Holiday stopped.

The wind slammed his door when he got out to set up the simple task. Agent Holiday's focus was that of an automaton;

neither dust devils nor tornadoes would deter him. Nothing ever stopped him from carrying out a mission.

In slowly modernizing Arab towns, camels could still be seen in the streets, saddled with goods. Cars dodged donkeys and goats wandering off the grassy centers of traffic circles. Agent Holiday ignored an advancing Bedouin goat herder in stained gray robes who was tending a dozen bleating black-and-white animals. Under the crook of his arm, a small, dirty, and disheveled child held on to his father's tall staff. A brown carpet of sand dust rose from the trampled earth as the Bedouins and their skinny flock began a counterclockwise search for grass in the circle.

The little boy watched Holiday park his shiny American car, hop out, and unwrap a package. When the paper fell away, the boy's eyes brightened. The man was holding a toy: a little friend for a small boy—a teddy bear.

Holiday paid no attention to the kid in the filthy brown *thobe* and skullcap; he never gave a thought to a child interfering with his mission. Bedouin nomads looking for handouts roamed the streets by the hundreds; he was used to them.

When the boy started across the circle toward the agent, his father, stuck with the unruly goats, could only yell at his son. "Hani! Hani! *'Amrikiin!*" The warning did not slow the child; he had his own mission. He wanted the teddy— wanted to hold it, pat the back of its fuzzy head, squeeze it to see if it could make a sound. The kid knew a grown man did not need a teddy bear. He did.

Hani tugged and pulled at the American's arm, shouting and pleading, "Please, mister, give, give, give me." He reached up for the bear, yelling in desert English. "Let me hold, mister. Give, give."

The boy would not listen to the big American's orders: "Go away, kid. Get outta here."

He wouldn't listen to his father either. This was the prize of all prizes. He'd never had a toy or a marble or a ball he hadn't shaped from trash-pile rubbish with his dung-stained hands. A soft stuffed bear with button eyes had never entered his imagination, but he needed a friend—even a toy friend.

Holiday knew nothing about teddy bears and less about kids. His heavyweight wrestler size dwarfed the boy; his massive hands and muscular body could have been a poster for a Las Vegas grudge match. Bulging muscles throbbed in his neck under a useless tie. Holiday's blue suit may have been the largest available but was still not big enough. The seams stretched, the buttons strained, and the pants fit like tights, soaked with sweat in the triple-digit heat. Struggling with a little kid added another ten degrees to his body temperature.

Holiday shoved the kid aside, opened the Chevy's rear door, knelt on the seat, and pushed the bear onto the shelf of the rear window. Like desert lightning, Hani slid under Holiday into the back seat and became engulfed in the agent's arms. Holiday yelled, "Shit, get out. You smell like a goat."

Cars slowed as astonished drivers watched a wrestling match develop between a crew cut–sporting American in a blue suit and a Bedouin child in his cotton thobe. None stopped.

Holiday could neutralize any enemy trying to kill him, but the little Bedouin had him reeling. His sense of honor would prevent him from killing the child, but his sense of duty was challenging his sense of honor. The boy grabbed the toy and scrambled for the opposite door. Holiday grabbed the boy's ankle and reached for the bear.

The boy's father, screaming and thrashing with the crook of his cane, proved more effective than the highly trained CIA agent. He caught his son and hauled him back into the center of the herd with swift swats of his staff. The old Bedouin wagged a finger at Holiday, turning his herd and his son back into the desert. The torn teddy bear appeared exhausted, flat on its back, resting on the rear deck of the Chevy.

Holiday locked the car, shuddered, and turned his back on the circle. He spun his sweat-saturated jacket off, waving it like a signal flag. A panel truck slowed, and the rear door opened. Holiday climbed in, and the panel truck took the exit to the airport.

The dust cloud of the Bedouin and his goats heading back into the desert had not settled when Sudakov's Lada crept past the black American Chevy. Sudakov rolled down the passenger window, which had fogged over from humidity, and blinked. His adrenaline pumping, he caught his image in the tiny rearview mirror. He saw a beaming Russian face, wide eyes dancing over a smile wide enough to bridge the Volga. Tears rolled down his pudgy cheeks, a constrained "*da*" formed at his lips. He had given Jack all the secrets he had plus files he had stolen, and now Jack had come through. The Lada turned onto the exit for the airport. He was going to America.

TWENTY-EIGHT

Little Goya

L ounging on Le Méridien's couches, robed Arabs sucked on hookahs, haggling prices for "deals of a lifetime" with Western businessmen in shiny gray sharkskin suits. Kuwait was the business center for the Emirates and the Eastern province of Saudi Arabia.

Waiting by the elevator doors, one man did not fit in with the robes or the suits. With a quick step, he got in front of Jack, offering his hand with an elfin smile, nodding toward a quiet area. "Sir, I'm Jalal Nassman. Honored to meet you. I bring the compliments of a heroic general, Mosheh Marwan. He said you'd be here, asked me to offer my humble services, such as they may be."

Momentarily stunned, Jack's curiosity switched to high gear. The small, beady-eyed man was unkempt; a day-old beard scrawled across the hollows of his cheeks drew attention to a monumental nose. His clothes looked like leftovers from a dirty war, a size too big. "General Marwan? How do you know him? Why would he ask you to offer me help?" Jack said, selecting a plush armchair facing the door. "Can't say I know him."

"Yes, you met only once, and he remembers it well. The general told me the circumstances of your meeting, asked me to help, ensure you have every opportunity to succeed in whatever you want to do."

Resting his elbows on his knees, Jack eyed the Goyaesque man and asked, "What is this about?"

The man lifted his head and spoke in a quiet voice. "A little background? My family has lived in Iran for generations, like the Marwan family. The general and I have a special relationship and quite important connections. We are part of a web of independence woven throughout the country. We function outside the Muslim world, although we are everywhere within it. Our community is strong. We survive, even prosper. We are, you could say, like a tribe."

Jack's mind flashed back to an instructor at MI6 who had warned against unexpected connections. "That means nothing to me, Mr. Nassman. What do you want?"

The man's black button vest partially covered a wrinkled white shirt, the cuffs rolled above the wrists. The sheen on his unpressed trousers reflected the light. He looked like an accountant in a bazaar. No one would mistake him for a Muslim or a tourist.

"I want simply to have a conversation with you. Give me just a few minutes of your time, please."

"Let's get a coffee," Jack said, nodding toward the bustling streets.

They walked in silence to a Lebanese café off the main road. The shop's shelves were stacked with honey-drenched phyllo *baklawas*, birds' nest pastries, and egg-shaped golden *maamouls*. Jack let sweet temptation pass, put his hand on Nassman's arm, and said, "The general is a friend of a friend. Now I want to know why he sent you. I'll be gone in seconds if you don't tell me what this is about."

"My favorite is the baklawa," Nassman said, pointing to pastries stacked on a mirrored tray. "The general said you would be cautious." He smiled; he was a happy puppy. "He sent me to help you get Farideh and her sister out of Iran."

Jack was dumbfounded.

Nassman continued. "The general and Farideh are part of our community, but our numbers have declined greatly. Some have gone to America, to Israel, even to Europe. Many are in prison. More are dead, like General Marwan's daughter. Her married name was Fatima Khaki, the mother of Farideh and Leah."

"How do you know about this?" Jack asked, feeling his face flush.

"Many years ago, General Marwan warned his daughter against marrying outside the faith, especially to a man like Mustafa Khaki. However, she was a young girl—headstrong, liked fast cars, parties, and travel. When she discovered her husband's business was killing people, she wanted to leave. But she couldn't; the girls were her life. She cried when she thought about what Khaki would do to them if she tried to take the girls and leave. He became enraged when Leah and Farideh were not paying enough attention to him. So ..."

Jack could have filled in the next sentence with words brimming with fire at the scum who had fathered the woman he loved. "Yes, I want to get Farideh out. Leah too. And I have other things I need to take care of in Tehran."

Nassman smiled. "Like getting her father's files?"

Shock, like a ruptured spring, uncoiled in Jack's body. He glared at Nassman, his feet frozen on the sidewalk as if cooling in fresh cement. Perspiration rained down his forehead, salting his eyes, blurring his focus on the small man in front of him, "What files? It's Farideh I want."

Nassman ignored the point. "You can't just fly to Iran anymore. A plan has been put together to get you back, with Khaki's approval. He arranged a medical evacuation for Leah, whose condition has gotten worse. He wants you and Farideh to escort her to a hospital in Europe. For some reason, he believes you are the person that can carry out his arrangements and get both girls out of his hair. Khaki has lost some of his power; he knows it, and he does not want two anchors like Leah and Farideh dragging his business down. He told Leah's nurse, Màasha, to make necessary arrangements to get you back into Iran, and then you and Màasha are to take Leah and Farideh and leave immediately.

"Believe me, Jack; this is your only chance to get Farideh out of Iran. The country is in total chaos. I'll take you to Basra, where we have friends among the Aramaic speakers—Christ's language. The Aramaics will help us cross into Iran, south of the battles going on between Iran and Iraq. From Basra we will go up to Saveh. My home is there; it's a pomegranate farm. You'll have to be hidden in the bed of my truck until we get to the farm.

"I know you are worried about Farideh, and you should be. Khaki will use her as a bargaining chip if he has to escape from Iran. And you must know one more thing."

"What is it?"

"Ali is planning to kill Khaki, steal his business, and take Farideh to Istanbul as his wife."

"Over my dead body."

Nassman glanced around without moving his head. "Let's walk. We could be watched."

"You're Mossad."

Nassman removed his nudging hand from the middle of Jack's back and said, "I'm but a simple pomegranate farmer." He grinned. "And a very good one. My Persian pomegranates went to the finest hotels in Paris, famous restaurants in London, and even New York. No more; my business has been destroyed, like my community." With his head bowed, his voice became somber in sadness. "Once, my community exceeded a hundred thousand people; now, twenty-five thousand, maybe less." He turned his hands palms-up and slapped the air. "Seventy-five thousand people gone. *Whoosh*—gone."

Nassman quickened his steps to keep up with Jack.

"You are Mossad."

"You could say I'm like a soldier. Our community does favors when Israel asks. Under the shah, SAVAK police protected us. They too are gone. The Islamists, the crazy ones, want to kill us, so we're hiding, like in Holocaust. My grandmother," Nassman wiped an arm over his face, his sleeves soaking up sweat and tears, "they cut." Two fingers slid across his throat.

Jack caught Nassman by the elbow, pulling him up on the curb as a convertible with four robed Kuwaitis bobbing to the music of Stevie Wonder sped through the crosswalk.

"Ha! You saved me. I owe you, and I always pay up, like getting you back to Farideh. Try it alone and you'll be dead the hour you arrive. Tehran is finished for you."

"Tell me something else, Mr. Nassman. I need to be sure of you."

The beaming smile returned. "You went to Lulu's with the lady who was in a wheelchair—a miracle."

Every muscle in Jack's body tightened. Nassman was real.

The world Hugh Ebanks had brought him into had changed his life forever; he was no longer in control—perhaps never had been. "Okay, you're clear, but I still don't know what you want," Jack said, his tone a bit more aggressive than he meant.

"It is not what I want; it is the deal you made. You proved yourself by getting the KGB guy to hand over information about Iran. Now you get Khaki's ledger, and we help get Farideh out. You give it to me to copy, and then we will give the file to the British embassy in Tel Aviv."

Jack's expression was intense. "Not going to happen, Mr. Nassman. We will copy the files and give them to your embassy in London."

Another puppy dog smile. No response.

Jack let the silence last a few seconds. "You probably know Khaki wanted me to get supplies and medicine for Leah. I arranged to have them sent from Germany, shipped through Oman along with the Fresenius dialysis equipment."

Nassman's smile disappeared, his forehead scrunched. "I'm afraid that plan was cancelled. Somebody got to your Omani supplier, roughed him up, and told him to forget the shipments."

Jack slammed his fist into his palm and came to a dead stop. "Impossible. Can't be. I paid a lot of money to ensure that shipment. Whaddya mean it's cancelled? Who cancelled it?"

The pomegranate farmer raised his eyebrows, grabbed Jack by the arm, pulled him closer, and whispered, "It was Hugh Ebanks."

"Ebanks? I'll kill him. I can't believe it."

Nassman let Jack take time to process, held his index finger within inches of his nose, and said, "Believe it. He's cunning and slimy—and you shouldn't trust him—but he knows what he's doing. He wants you back in Iran to finish the job. The plan is in place for you to get Leah and Farideh out of Iran, but that's only half your deal."

Jack shook his head, pushed Nassman's hand off his shoulder, folded his arms, and said, "You're crazy. This isn't how it's supposed to be."

"Nothing ever is, my friend. That's why we all fight. Right or wrong, we fight because things are not what we think they should be. The real problem is the other guys— the Ebankses, the Palestinians, the IRA—they fight too, and for the same reason. It's complicated, and it will never end. Ebanks played his dirty trick because he wants you back in Tehran to finish his mission. Our 'company' agreed to work with him so we have the supplies Leah needs to travel."

"It's my mission, not his."

"Forget it, my friend. Getting the ledger is his mission, and you're a tool. He just wants the ledger. Canceling the medication was his way of getting you to go back. He doesn't care about Farideh, Leah, me, or even you. But I care, and so do you. We'll go back together, we'll get Farideh and Leah out, and we'll get the ledger. Then we'll deal with Ebanks. We leave today."

A hole in Jack's heart ached for attention. He longed for love, for recognition. He wanted what everyone else had: someone who cared for him, someone he could care for, some Light Brigade he could lead to victory. He wanted Farideh, Leah, the ledger—he wanted it all. He wanted it to be over. MI6 had complimented him on how well he had handled Sudakov. That praise had already been buried in the cemetery of compliments.

The loud rap on the door of his hotel room would not be room service. In the doorway, a tall, white-robed Arab stood with a bag in hand. Sabah had found a forgotten suitcase in the hotel's basement; he brought it into Jack's room and began a mini lecture, handing him an envelope.

"Got your message. You decided to go camping in the desert? Be careful, Mr. Jack. It's very cold at night. Sleep by the belly of your camel. Don't go alone; it is dangerous. Worse, it is *majnoon*—crazy. You may be strong, and Allah will protect you, but there is more danger in the desert than there is sand." Sabah's wrinkled brow made Jack think he was deeply troubled.

Jack dropped the beaten-up suitcase, handed Sabah a ten-dinar note, and said, "Don't worry, my good friend; I'll be back in a couple of weeks."

Sabah bowed, backing out of the room. "*Shokran*; I will keep your things safe until you return. Allah be with you."

Jack looked down at the men-only hotel pool, his thoughts still on the fifty-three men locked up in the embassy whose lives had to be miserable, and felt a quiver of relief that the women had been released.

Jack refocused his mind to coalesce around the mission. The intended result was clear; the method to accomplish the result was not. He opened the envelope.

> You will have only six days, seven at most, to get in and out of the country. President Carter may take action soon, and when he does, all non-Muslims will be killed.
>
> Furlong assured me you can trust Nassman.
>
> C

In a musty hall at MI6 over civilized tea and crumpets, an agent had once given Jack a tip: "When you meet a contact, they will say something to confirm who they are—something no outsider could know. When this happens, 99 percent of the time, you can trust them; but then there is the 1 percent … devilish bit, that 1 percent."

Nassman drove up to the hotel; he barely even slowed down enough for Jack to jump in. His decrepit '56 Ford crossed the Kuwait/Iraq border less than two hours after leaving Kuwait City. "That was easy, Jack. We may not be so lucky crossing from Iraq to Iran—some fighting between us and the Iraqis further north."

"I'm still wondering what side you're on."

Nassman only smiled.

The car turned onto a rutted road off the highway, east of Basra. On one side, secondhand stores, paint stalls, and car repair shops faced junkyards lining the banks of the Euphrates River. Nassman dodged a goat and wheeled right into a puddle of mud in front of Samir's Body Shop. A heavy door to a car bay slid open, and a double-bellied Iraqi in a greasy undershirt waved the Ford in.

"See, Jack, there's my pomegranate truck. It arrived from the farm in Saveh last night and just made the last delivery." Nassman acted like a schoolboy getting a passing grade. "The pomegranates would have been packed up to here." He raised his hand over the height of the truck's cab. "Our trip up to Saveh will take a long time. We'll drive all night. Get in the back." Nassman loosely tied an oily black tarp to the top rails. "This will give you some shade."

"Shove it, Nassman; it's pitch black."

The truck was filthy, the narrow ribs of its bed too close for Jack to find a comfortable spot. A half dozen dented, broken pomegranates squashed into soggy red pulp would be Jack's only cushion. "All night? All night in the back? Crazy." Jack shook his head in frustration. It had no effect on Nassman.

"Once we're outside, in the country, I'll bring you up to the cab, but for now, get in and lie down. Samir will cover you with another tarp until we get across the border into Iran." Samir yanked open his shop door. Nassman ground into gear and raced out, splashing the truck through deep mud puddles, bouncing his passenger like a sack of rags.

Chunks of Jack's positive mindset crumbled amid broken crates, eviscerated pomegranates, and soggy tarps as the pickup truck left the washboard road for a potholed highway. The truck picked up speed, rolling dented pomegranates like baseballs between the ribs, smashing some in a stinking mass against the tailgate. Nassman's instructions were stern: "Stay under the tarp until we get to the open road."

At the border crossing, an Iraqi guard announced he needed to see inside and told Nassman to pull back the tarp. Nassman jumped out quickly, his plump Persian fruits cradled in both hands. The guard accepted the "gifts" and waved the truck into the three-hundred-meter space between Iraq and Iran—no-man's-land.

On the Iranian side, border guards waved for Nassman to stop. A sergeant edged up to the driver's side of the vehicle, sniffing like a tracking dog. In the back of the pickup, 110-degree heat had cooked the broken fruit into a smelly, putrid slime. Jack heard the sergeant bump against the side of the truck and saw his hand begin to lift the tarp. In a split second, the tarp was slammed shut and Jack heard the guard shout, "*Iydefiqu!*" It did not need translation. The guard told Nassman to move along, fast.

Jack's thoughts about the romance and adventure of his life as a spy were wilting on the filthy floorboard of an old, rickety pickup. The truck cleared the border in minutes and passed a roundabout to take the road to Saveh. In the back, Jack's mind played a game of odds. He was shouting, cursing, and berating imaginary mullahs even though he knew no one could hear him. "I've pissed my legs, destroyed my body, tormented my soul, and the next person who pulls away the tarp may cut off my head. This is insane. I am lost. No one will ever know what happened. I won't even have a widow." In the hours it took to drive northeast from the bottom of western Iran, Jack fought and defeated despair. He concentrated on his missions, Farideh, and MI6, in that order.

In the darkness, sounds of overloaded trucks, horns blasting in anger from a distance, and the heavy thud of mortar shells rupturing off the mountains tried to syncopate the flapping of the tarp that covered his solitary confinement. Nassman said they would pass convoys of Iranian Army trucks carrying young men to their deaths on the plains of southern Iraq. They would pass the same number of trucks in convoys heading in the opposite direction, toward Tehran. They would be carrying remains.

Nassman looked for lights in both directions, saw none, and pulled over onto a berm and said, "Jack, get in front." Patrols increased with dawn. They had to be quick and keep moving.

"Hurry up," said Nassman.

Jack scraped accumulated muck off his clothes and plopped into the passenger seat. Nassman pulled back onto the road. Mud puddles joined with other mud puddles, turning the old road into a river. Villagers would be out in the morning to scoop and shape the mud into building blocks for houses that would stand until the next earthquake returned them to the earth. The process, repeated over centuries, would continue forever.

In the dull light, they could see faint shapes along the road—ancient abandoned forts, half crumbled, their stubbed towers silent sentinels protesting long-gone armies, wind, rain, and the inevitable judgment of time.

Nassman mumbled in monotone as he fought the mesmerizing drive.

"You're praying," Jack said. "In Hebrew?"

"Don't tell Allah," Nassman laughed. "We'll be at the farm soon. You'll get instructions. You'll accomplish your mission … might even stay alive."

Jack instinctively turned to catch Nassman's expression. "You guys are all alike."

From the moment they'd met in Kuwait, Nassman had been dropping tidbits of information, but he could not be pressed.

Jack tried again, probing. "Have you served?"

"You ask like a Jew, and I know you're not. Yes, five years, IDF—Israeli Defense Forces." Nassman turned pensive. "Five years and six days. I was to be discharged on the fifth of June in '67, but we had a short war."

Only windshield wipers broke the silence. *Scrape, squish, scrape, squish.*

"You guys ran over the Arabs. I remember," Jack said.

Nassman clenched his fist, pumped it, and then became somber. "Yeah, and we got Jerusalem back, but we lost some solid people."

Jack respected Nassman's silence and change of subject.

"I'll tell you the basics. Khaki is afraid of his brothers in Islam who say there is a cancer in his house and his business will be protected only if he gets rid of the Jews in the household. He doesn't know there are three. Leah's nurse is one of us."

"Who are the other two?"

"Farideh and Leah."

"But he's their father, a Muslim; only their mother was Jewish. They're half Jewish."

"If the mother is a Jew, her children are Jews. If the father is Jewish, but not the mother, the children are not Jews." Another lesson in spiritual culture for Jack to absorb.

Jack's concern for the girls was growing. He put a hand on Nassman's shoulder and asked, "When will Ali make his move? He seems to be running the show."

"You're smart, and you're right. He uses the girls to manage Khaki. He is a very bad guy. If he takes over the business, he will become the most dangerous man in the world, and no one will be able to stop him from taking Farideh for himself."

Jack shuddered and said, "As I told you, he'll have to kill me first."

A narrow beam of light split the night. Nassman slapped Jack's hip and yelled, "Get in the back. A roadblock." Another intense beam switched on. Night became day.

"Three hundred meters. I can't stop here or they'll shoot." Nassman slid the truck's rear window open and yelled, "Move!" He pushed in the cigarette lighter. "Squeeze, squeeze! Get under the tarp. I know those guys. Fast, Jack! Go, push, squeeze!"

Jack knelt on the cracked plastic-covered seat, stuck his arms through the narrow window, pulled on the rails, and pushed from his knees. The top half of his body hung in the rain, his hands sliding on the slimy, wet wall of the truck bed, looking for leverage. He writhed, tossed, pushed, cursed, and squirmed. He never heard the cigarette lighter pop out.

Jack felt the red-hot lighter sting his ass like a wasp and shot through the window. While the truck slowed, Jack stewed under stinking tarps, holding his breath while Nassman, singing in Farsi, feathered the clutch until the truck bucked to a stop.

Jack knew only a few Farsi words, but with his understanding of inflection, semantics, and language, he knew he was hearing friendly young voices—those of teenagers.

Nassman returned a greeting. "Salam Bhaman." There were three speakers: two teens and Bhaman, probably the father.

Jack heard Nassman get out, speak to the trio, and pop back in. The truck began to roll, and Jack slid the window open. "You'll pay for that, Nassman. Nobody burns an Irishman's ass."

"Oh, didn't know you were Irish."

"What did they want? Was that a guard post?"

"Yeah, they were army. Bhaman lives in the village; I know him. Don't worry. A couple of pomegranates and a fistful of rials did the trick—tolls, they call it. He told me patrols are active in the area, so stay down until we get off the main road. Every province crossing is being closed. We're almost there. It's about thirty kilometers to my farm."

Nassman turned onto the gravel path to his farm. The truck rumbled across a cattle grid and pulled to a stop.

"Okay, Jack, hop out and get back in the front. The barn is just over the hill."

Jack slopped over the side rail, engaging in a Saint Vitus dance, shaking pomegranate crap off his brutalized body. An intense downpour saturated his clothes, dripping pomegranate bits onto his sneakers. "You're not Mossad, Nassman," he shouted in Nassman's window. "You report to Lucifer himself!"

"You're funny, Jack. Get in. My guys need at least an hour to get you ready, and we're almost there. I'll explain later."

The rain thinned enough for the truck's hood to turn the rain to steam. The truck splashed on and then turned onto a gouged and rutted tractor path of a road.

"You'll have time to hose off and get ready. My team is waiting; they know exactly what to do. Don't worry."

In the hostility of the rain, the pomegranate mud, the heat, and the neighborhood, Jack thought of Alfred E. Neuman, the cartoon character who faced danger at every turn and refuted it with a defensive "What, me worry?"

Nassman kept up the chatter. "There are other things. Farideh may have changed."

Jack grabbed for the steering wheel, pushing Nassman's shoulder against the seat back. "Changed? What do you mean she changed? What's going on? Stop the truck."

Nassman kept his speed, pushed Jack off, and said, "Easy, son, easy. Maybe she's getting nervous. Maybe she's afraid. Ali may be the problem. You need to concentrate on the mission."

Jack did not completely trust Nassman; but he did trust Farideh and did not believe she could have changed. He had to get to her. "Do you have enough of the kidney drugs to travel to Europe?"

"The drugs, yes; the equipment too. Màasha is taking care of that."

The bolero staccato of the rain numbed Jack's feelings about killing the man who could become his father-in-law.

A litany of wrongs grew in Jack's mind: the Revolutionary Guard holding American hostages, Hugh forcing him to get the ledger, MI6's plan to neutralize Khaki and Ali, and, worst of all, seeds of doubt about Farideh.

Nassman lifted one finger off the steering wheel, pointing ahead. "That's the farm where you'll be prepared for the trip in the ambulance. A man from our community, Ohr, will be waiting to bring you up to date."

THIRTY

A Pomegranate Farm in Iran

Arriving at Nassman's farm was the end of a ride from hell. The truck slid to a stop under the overhang of the barn's roof. Lights reflected over the tops of small windows in the old barn, from which voices were getting louder. In the foggy gray rain, someone pushed the barn doors open. Jack was as apprehensive as he'd been on the day he first walked into the headquarters of MI6 in London.

"This is like a set for a movie, Nassman; is this place real?"

Inside the long barn, among tractors and crates of pomegranates, a white ambulance gleamed like a dove of peace. The ambulance sported a red crescent above Farsi script painted on its side panels. It had emergency light bars in front and back, oversize tires, and bullhorn sirens mounted on the front fenders.

Nassman grinned, slapping the shoulders of a couple workers heading to his fields. "There's the ambulance."

Jack stalled his rush to the hose to look inside the ambulance. It was perfect for getting everyone out of the Khaki compound: Leah on the gurney, Farideh in the front seat next to the driver with Nassman next to her, and the nurse in the medical jump seat. No room for him?

Nassman spoke as if he had read Jack's mind. "You will be riding under the gurney from Khaki's compound to the airport. Nothing to worry about, Jack." A devilish gleam twinkled in Nassman's eyes as he continued. "From here you will ride on the gurney like a wounded soldier from the front lines heading for a hospital in Tehran. You will have to be bloody and only partially conscious."

"Bloody?"

"We'll take care of that."

In the early-morning dampness of the barn, a shiver brought Jack's imagination to attention.

Nassman raised his hand like a tour guide and waved to an academic-looking man whose yarmulke was held bravely in place by brown bobby pins. The two embraced like battlefield comrades, mumbling prayer-like into the hollows of each other's ears.

"Okay, guys, hug time is over. Who are you?" Jack asked.

"Eliyahu Sternberg to some. Persians call me Ohr Kaman. I am at your service, sir," he said. Sternberg-Kaman steepled his hands and bowed.

"Jack Devlin."

"We know who you are; we're on the same side." He pointed to people at the far end of the long barn and said, "That's Leah's nurse; you know her. She came to help the transfer of the wounded soldier."

"Wait a minute." Jack's irritation burst into intolerance. "This is almost like musical chairs ... same characters, different locations." Jack grabbed Nassman's arms, pulled him face-to-face, lowered his voice, and looked into his eyes, searching for a soul. "You and I have been together for hours, and I know less about you now than I did when we met." Jack turned to Ohr. "I'm not being given a complete story."

"You're right," said Ohr, looking over his shoulder. "This lady will help you understand."

Màasha walked toward the men, her knees poking a crunchy black skirt, eyes fixed; hers was the stride of a purposeful nurse in a crisp uniform. The sleeves of her neck-high, black blouse billowed to double-button white cuffs. Starched white purposeless suspenders climbed over her breasts and crossed her shoulders to connect to a wide midriff belt.

"Màasha."

"I'm also known as Rebekkah in my community; Màasha is my business name. We have come up with a plan to smuggle you back to Khaki's compound. All Americans are Satans in Iran, which is the reason for the disguise."

Nassman moved to stand next to Màasha, placing a comforting hand on her arm. "Màasha's father came from Iran to fight with us against the Egyptians. I was next to him in the Sinai Desert. A dog ran at us strapped with explosives. He threw himself on the dog. Saved six Israeli lives, including mine. It was on the fifth day."

The nurse rested her head on Nassman's shoulder, reflecting that people who live in uncaring surroundings suffer quietly; they cry inside, where only their heart is aware. Jack felt for her; he recognized her heartache. In the predawn hour, on a Persian pomegranate farm in a warehouse big enough for a blimp, Màasha, Ohr, and Nassman shared love and legacy. Jack had his team.

Ohr hustled two farmhands to a short stack of boxes with instructions to pack everything under the gurney.

"These are the supplies I need for Leah," said Màasha, "and they are scarce. We paid a lot of money to smuggle them in; we barely have enough for our trip. The shipments Mr. Khaki ordered never arrived."

The workers showed each package to the nurse. In a professional monotone, she identified each one like a pilot with a checklist. "Dialyzers, okay. Dumbbell filters, right. Single-use tubing, yes. Batch dialysate, saline IV fluid in one-liter bags … okay, these are what I need.

"You know, Mr. Devlin, in Tehran she could have a transplant. There are two fresh kidneys on every crazy motorcyclist racing through the streets, and Mr. Khaki could easily kill one, but that is not what he wants. He doesn't trust Muslim hospitals."

"Is Leah okay to travel?"

"She is close to the end stages of the disease. If she misses a day and her potassium gets too high, she will have to be hooked up to the machine constantly. Her blood pressure must be checked every fifteen minutes. I have another nurse with her now."

The workers loaded the final packages and locked the gurney to the vehicle's floor, ready for its next passenger—Jack.

"Nassman, let's go over our route: timing, expectations, arrival at Khaki's compound, loading, and getting to the airport. I want to know every detail, every hurdle, and your plan for resolving any conflicts." Jack thought his MI6 terminology placed him in control. He was wrong.

"Take your clothes off and sit on the gurney please, Mr. Devlin," ordered Màasha.

"What the hell are you talking about?" Jack stuffed his hands in his pockets in defiance.

"Shorts, socks, shoes, Jack. We are losing time. We have to get you ready for whatever interrogations may come up on our trip. Remember: I'm a nurse."

She beckoned the farmhands to help Jack. They were just like hammam workers getting him out of his shoes and onto his back. His eyes bugged, his teeth weaponized. The farmhands immobilized him in three seconds.

Màasha scissored half his shirt and started on his pants. "You're not wearing jeans like most Americans, so we'll let you keep some of your clothes on. Remember: you're a battlefield hero returning from Iraq, and we're getting you back to Tehran for surgery."

Nassman stood over him and said, "Sorry; we need to give you something that'll put you to sleep for a while. If we get stopped, police interrogators at control points will find you unresponsive. We'll cut into your earlobes—they bleed a lot—just in case some guard wants to examine you up close. We have goat's blood to soak into the bandages that'll cover your eyes. It smells bad, but you do too."

The farmhands held his head in a viselike lock. Jack felt a knife slice through his ears.

"You're okay," said Màasha watching warm blood flow down his neck. "Earlobes produce lots of blood, but they heal—usually."

He did not see the needle coming. It led to an IV tube hanging on a short rack.

"What is that? You guys are poisoning me."

"It's only saline; you have to look like a wounded hero. No talking until we get inside Khaki's compound."

It was not just a simple saline solution, as a fog began to sweep over him.

Ohr took the wheel. Nassman, in a white doctor's coat, sat next to him. Nurse Màasha sat in the medic seat next to their "hero."

The farmhands pulled on heavy chains, raising the barn door for the gleaming white ambulance. Its red lights revolving, the siren's low wail pierced the air; the mission was in motion.

The ambulance rumbled over the cattle grid, heading to the main road. "From here, about two hundred kilometers to Tehran," Nassman announced.

Jack heard him but could not distinguish between hallucinatory dreams and the fog of his reality. He felt blood still flowing from his ear, running under the back of his neck, sopping into gauze wraps. The weight of congealed goat's blood pulled on the bandages covering his face. Màasha said they would be tightened if revolutionaries at a roadblock approached for a closer inspection. He would be semiconscious, unable to answer questions. The last thing he heard was Nassman's opinion that the stupid sentries would not probe Jack's bloody face or ask questions. They would be revolted and would wave the three Jews and the Irishman through their barricades, praise Allah.

The ambulance crawled through the unpredictable mountain fog on the narrow road to Tehran.

Jack's groggy mind began to clear. "I'm taking off these stinking bandages," he slurred. He grabbed the IV tubes, slid his hand along the plastic to the tape holding the needle, and yanked it out of his arm. Fresh blood spurted on nurse Màasha's white suspenders. Jack stretched his hand to wipe the blood. Màasha slapped him hard on the side of his head, boxed his ears and retrieved a roll of wet gauze to clean her uniform.

"Selfish American. You're on a mission to get Leah out of this horrible country, so don't screw it up. Do you know what'll happen to you if we're caught?"

Jack said, "I'll be shot."

"Do you know what'll happen to me? You don't want to know."

A t the edge of the city, pigeons squawked and flew off, their air space invaded by the wail of the siren, which attracted little respect from drivers in the horn-blowing traffic. Tehran's trucks, buses, cars, and burros ignored ambulance sirens, never pulling over. Their logic held that if they were not in the ambulance, why bother?

The Saveh Highway ended in the streets of an industrial complex south of the city, half an hour away from the Khaki compound. The streets were clogged with heavy traffic as workers returned to their offices following late-afternoon lunch.

Straining to come out of his fog, Jack felt a deep, soulful excitement to see Farideh after being apart. He had stuffed Nassman's comments about her and Ali, knowing in his heart she had not changed.

At the top of Nasibi Street, the twenty-foot-high gates parted. Ohr turned off the siren and gunned the ambulance into the courtyard, around the great stone mansion, and downhill toward a stable behind the multicar garage. A black-suited guard walking in quick steps alongside the ambulance, shouting orders in Farsi, directed Ohr to the right. Ohr followed, until the suit sliced a finger across his throat. Ohr cut the engine. The cavernous garage had a double depth for a Rolls Royce, a black Saipa pickup, and a shiny new 1979 Cadillac limousine. Wreckage of a red Ferrari waited in a corner for a miracle.

Màasha handed Jack a gray turtleneck, pants, and workman boots. She removed his bandages and directed him to a shower in the corner of the garage. She then jumped out of the ambulance and caught up with the black suit, commanding him to get the supplies out and then clean it for its next patient, Leah. Màasha would start the dialysis treatment immediately. It had been three days since Leah's last treatment; she would have to be on dialysis until they left for the airport.

The Turkish bodyguard snapped to attention when Ali walked into the garage. Jack had just finished getting changed, Ohr had disappeared, and Nassman's head was buried under the hood of the ambulance. Ali spotted Jack and said, "You are back, Mr. Jack."

"Hello, Ali." Jack avoided a handshake.

"Boss wants to see you," said Ali. The generics stood still; Nassman and Ohr moved together to stand next to Jack.

Nassman spoke with Ali in Farsi. Their conversation seemed friendly enough. "Jack, nothing to worry about. It's about getting everyone out of the country tonight. The medical evacuation plane will be waiting," said Nassman.

Ali nodded.

A whisper from Ohr sounded like a question: "Mazel tov?"

Ali sent the Jew a scowl.

"Okay, guys," said Jack. "Going to talk with Khaki. Need to get to the airport in plenty of time. Make sure the ambulance is ready."

"Mazel tov," said Ohr.

Khaki had paid in advance for Leah's supplies. If he knew about the cancellation, he would be enraged. Jack walked into the dark-paneled office holding his breath. He extended his hand to keep the squat weapons merchant to his left and seated—an MI6 tactic. Jack looked down on the perspiring, overweight, sickly cologned Persian and exhaled.

Two bodyguards stood at attention; Ali took his place between them.

"Allah be praised, Mr. Jack, you are back," Khaki said. "A thousand welcomes to the only American in my country not in chains. I am happy for you. Welcome, come sit with me." Jack braced to have his hands squeezed by the rings Khaki wore on three fingers of his small right hand. The obnoxious diamond ring on his thumb outdid all three.

On the cordovan-covered table between the chairs, a photo in a golden frame caught Jack's eye. Khaki followed Jack's gaze and pointed out that the bemedaled general in full dress regalia was his father. He was standing next to a man in a wheelchair with a blanket over his legs. "That's Franklin Delano Roosevelt. Every American president has been a friend to my family until Jimmy Carter. He is no friend of mine; he is no friend to Iran."

"Iran has few friends, Mr. Khaki," Jack said, sliding into the leather chair. He looked Khaki in the eye and began winging it. "Sorry the Omanis could not ship Leah's dialysis supplies; I'll arrange payment—"

Khaki raised his palm. "No, stop, Mr. Jack; you are an honorable man. My bank confirmed yesterday that you returned all my money. You've done better for me than I did for you. When we first talked about getting your money back, I did not make the arrangements. This time, everything is different; money will be sent to your account, all arranged, Mr. Jack. I knew you would have very little chance in getting the supplies into Iran; border restrictions have tightened. That is why I arranged for you to get back here—so you could escort Leah to London."

Jack realized that Hugh must have returned the money; no one else could have arranged the transfer. That move might have saved his life. *What game was Hugh playing?* Jack hid his astonishment but was not surprised Khaki was taking credit for circumstances about which he knew nothing. Jack sat back, grinned, and said, "Of course. We must move quickly. You've completed the arrangements?"

"Yes, everything is ready, Mr. Jack, just as I planned. It was I who sent the nurse to get the supplies from the Jews in Saveh. They were doing my bidding, getting you through the Revolutionary Guard posts and back to my office."

"They are very good people; I would not be here if it were not for them."

"Perhaps, but one word from me and those Jews would be in their tombs."

Jack liked Khaki blurting out his feelings. Prejudice is the voice of insecurity.

Khaki continued. "This country is changing by the hour. If I don't get Leah out soon, we may never get her out. It's a problem for me."

"Farideh will be able to help Leah after she gets a transplant. It will prove what a good father you really are, having made all these arrangements."

Khaki turned to catch Ali's eye.

"Sorry, Jack; there's been a little change," said Ali.

Jack froze, his teeth clenched. Ali's goons moved to the heavily curtained vestibule door. They stood motionless, all eyes fixed on Jack, whose heart said the "little change" would have to do with Farideh. He breathed her name, his lips moving to make a sound he debated making. He controlled a shudder and said, "Farideh?"

As if the mention of her name was a summons, the goons bowed their heads. Each drew his side of the curtains open. Jack was stunned. Farideh's head was bowed. A black cloth mask veiled her cheeks, and her hands fell through midnight folds of a cold, black chador, her fingertips gently touching her garment. The long gown draped shapelessly to her feet. She stood perfectly still.

Jack rose and braced the backs of his knees on the leather arm of his chair, speechless. Khaki remained in his emperor's chair, spreading wide his thick arms to display and embellish everyone's attention on his oldest daughter, who stood like a netherworld goddess in the archway.

No one spoke.

In the continuing silence, the goddess in black began to sway. Her body moved as though the chador covered a cloud, billowing silently, like a gentle evening wind waving heather in a field. In an instant, the goons dropped the curtains and she disappeared.

Jack's mouth was dry, his mind grasping but refusing to believe what he saw. The girl of his dreams had changed. Her eyes had been nearly closed, offering no twinkle, no spark—nothing. Her fashionably thin shaped eyebrows were gone. Farideh was adorned in the style required by the Revolution: that of a subservient Muslim woman with no voice, no personality, and no independence—just another anonymous body covered in the black crepe of the anonyms. Nassman's warning had been too mild.

Jack recognized the drama was for him. He looked hard at Ali and then turned to face Khaki.

"Jack, please, sit back, relax. Tea?"

Jack did not answer.

Khaki sipped from his cerulean blue cup, peered over the rim, and said, "Farideh has decided to marry Ali."

A cloudburst of anger drenched Jack to his soul. Khaki's statement was a blur—not real, not possible. Jack could not wrap his head around what was happening. He stared at Ali. He knew he was looking at the devil. Ali must have promised to provide Khaki safe passage to Turkey and protection from the beheading radical Islamists; Jack understood Ali wanted Khaki's empire. Khaki's daughter was just the ribbon on the package.

Ali spoke up. "We will have our marriage blessed at the Blue Mosque in Istanbul. Mr. Jack, you'll be invited of course."

Every muscle in Jack's body tensed, his heart torn in pieces. Another dictum from his mentor at MI6 flashed before him: "Disarm surprise by controlling emotion."

Maintaining his composure, he said to the servant, "Tea, please. Lemon, no sugar." He then turned to Ali, smiled, and said, "Congratulations, you're a very lucky man."

"I am, my friend. The wedding will be at the end of the month."

Ali would have bargained for Farideh, but she loved Jack, and he knew it. She would not change her mind, her heart, or her passion. When Farideh had exited through the doors held open by Ali's thugs, she made a motion no one else would have noticed. She leaned toward the sunlit parlor, turned slightly, and then inclined her head, just a little.

Through the diaphanous veil, Jack saw her exquisite profile; their eyes met. In that moment, he saw her desperation. He had mimicked the move, inclining his head, just a little. The moment would stay with him forever. His heart thundered back from a cave of despair and doubt. Farideh had found a way to let him know she was still his.

There was no doubt Farideh was forced to agree to the marriage. It would have been a life-or-death threat. He silently promised that Farideh would not go to Istanbul and neither would he. Ali might—in a box.

THIRTY-TWO

The Qajar Room

Nassman had informed Jack that someday the Revolutionary Guard would kill Khaki for being an apostate; they would put him on trial for marrying a Jew. It would have to be soon or the apostate would flee the country. Khaki would not survive in Islamic Iran, weapons or not.

He had the ruthless, narcissistic bullying characteristics MI6 had described. Khaki handing his daughter over to Ali in exchange for protection from the Sunni militants and their head-chopping teenage acolytes would not bring a tear to his eye. With Ali's connections, he could protect his boss, arrange passage to Istanbul, and continue the trade. Buyers wanted guns.

Jack emptied his teacup and placed it on the table.

Ali spoke. "I have personal business to discuss with Mr. Khaki in the conference room." He motioned toward the circular staircase leading to the lower rooms. "Please, relax, Mr. Jack. I have a few things to discuss with you after Mr. Khaki and I finish. Go downstairs and have some refreshments. I will find you later, and we'll talk."

On his last visit to "Khakiland," Farideh had taken him to the Qajar Room, which was lined with images painted on glass. The viewing side showed subjects like military officers of the dynasty in full military regalia. Farideh had removed one painting of a resplendent sovereign to show him the reverse side of the glass's layered kaleidoscope of color. When she stretched to hang the painting back on its hook, he joked that the painting was like a person—captivating on the surface, but on the other side an ugly blob.

Jack opened the door to the Qajar Room. There, reflected in the framed glass, he saw her.

"My darling." Farideh's fingers stole the veil from her face as she moved toward him. Jack swept Farideh off her feet in an embrace, triggering a thirst their love could never quench. She leaned back, staring at him, her warm brown eyes reddened but happy. Jack's lips met hers, and for the moment, the world was bliss.

"Lock the door and the service entrance behind the fireplace." She took Jack's hand, led him to a couch, and raised a finger to her lips.

Jack had a hundred questions but decided questions should wait.

"I have my father's ledger. I got it when they left for the conference room."

Jack's admiration for Farideh soared. "I know of a company in Washington who would hire you in a minute."

She slipped her veil back in place, concentrating on her surroundings, on noises, but still on Jack. "We have no time."

The only visible feature of Farideh's body were her eyes. Her head tilted back slightly, and the black silk did not stick to her lips when she said, "Jack, I'm terrified I'll be caught."

"Go to Leah, where you'll be safe. The plan is in motion. Look." Jack pulled back the window drape and pointed to the ambulance. "It's for Leah and you."

"How can this work? How can we all escape? My father will kill you; Ali will kill all of us. We have no guns. Even if we did, I can't kill anyone—especially my father. I just want to be rid of him—rid of his terrible friends." She sobbed into Jack's chest.

"We'll be all right. I don't have to tell you not to worry, but I will. Màasha's friends Nassman and Ohr are here, and we are your team. We'll get you and Leah out of here, safe from Ali—safe from worry." When he said the words, it sounded easy; he knew it was not. Jack folded her into his arms, whispered, "I love you, Farideh," and then watched her disappear behind the fireplace. There was purity in the thought of sharing their love together, fighting for their freedom, and fighting for their future, sharing the challenge and the victory.

Tehran locals loved to compare their hilly capitol to San Francisco or Rome. The Khaki compound was on one of the higher hills, with enviable views of the Tochal Mountains. Behind the house, a tight wall of eucalyptus trees climbed defiantly into Tehran's smog. The trees towered over the fifty-meter-long narrow building that housed a garage on one end, staff living quarters on the other.

Jack found Nassman and Ohr crouching next to the pickup.

"Farideh's all right; I told her to get ready to leave as soon as Leah's dialysis is finished. We need to shape our strategy. We have one chance to pull this off and get on the plane," Jack said.

"What happened in the house?" Nassman asked.

"Details later; right now we gotta figure out our next steps."

Near the wrecked Ferrari, a long table became the center of their war room. "We've got to speed things up and get Farideh out of Ali's reach." He sketched a floor plan of the compound, pointing out the office, the Qajar Room, Leah's location on the ground floor, and the bedrooms on the top.

Ohr spread out a map of the city and tapped on the location of the final objective, Mehrabad Airport. "No way to take shortcuts, guys; we will have to take the main road all the way to Mehrabad, dealing with checkpoints when they come up. Maybe they'll just let an ambulance pass through."

The elfin smile returned with Nassman's sardonic laugh. "Just say we have an American in the back and he's trying to catch a flight."

"Every day your presence gives me life," Leah said. "You have loved me so. You make me want to dance, to sing, to fly away to a land of love where money and power have disappeared into a purgatory of regret. When you gently kiss me on the forehead, the tears you see are only little drops of joy. I am so grateful to you, Farideh; you make me believe that I may have my own life someday, that I may get well—even find love."

Farideh took her sister's hands and told Leah she was not alone and never would be. They would be a part of each other in a way Leah could not have imagined. Farideh hated secrets, but the test results would not be shared with Leah until they got to London. Leah would have a chance at living a normal life; she would receive a perfectly healthy kidney—her sister's.

Farideh looked at Màasha. "Jack said we need to be on the plane by ten o'clock, not one second later."

"Right. This procedure has to continue for another hour. We can make it. We will be ready by nine."

Leah asked, "Will Father be okay? Will he join us?"

Farideh thought about how they had lost their mother, how the country they loved was no more, and how their friends had all run away. She felt they were like virgins in a colosseum of gladiators, but they would win. Love can be forgiving, even if misguided. When it is given freely, there are no conditions; and in the souls of their beings, the sisters had some love for their father; even Farideh had a little for him.

Màasha lightly touched Farideh's elbow, urging her to let Leah rest.

Farideh bent over her sister and said, "We love the good things about our father, and we will have him with us when God is ready."

THIRTY-THREE

Two-Wheeled Brigade

J ack looked through the garage window at the trees lining the slope as dusk brought the lights of Tehran into relief. Bursts of yellow and gold reflected on landscapes still wet from late-afternoon showers.

Kicking a dented Ferrari fender out of his way, Nassman said, "We don't have much time. I received messages from Tel Aviv. Trivelpiece wants the entire crew to evacuate Iran immediately. Intel says the hostages will be dispersed within a few days. Trivelpiece has already called in all agents working in Iran. When the Americans get this information, they will take immediate steps to rescue the hostages."

Jack said, "This is nuts. Tehran would be the last place on earth for me, an American, to be during any attempt to rescue the hostages."

"Can't worry about that now. We have to get that ledger."

"Farideh has it."

Shocked, Jalal Nassman lifted his head and fixed a hard stare at Jack. His jaw clenched; the stubble on his chin tightened as his arms folded. "What's going on, Jack?" he balanced his voice on the razor edge that separates challenge from question. Nassman was capable of turning into a battlefield warrior in an instant.

"Easy, friend. The real reason Farideh's father gave Ali permission to marry her was in return for his safe passage to Istanbul. She is trying to escape from both of them. She snuck into her father's office to get the ledger for me."

Nassman, relieved, turned on his elfin smile. "Ohr and I have some news for you. Ohr hung our star on the front gate of the compound. Mr. Khaki will be having company in a few minutes." He smirked like a kid holding all the marbles.

"The Star of David? You hung the Star of David on the gate? That's insane. What're you guys doing?"

"You'll see," said Nassman.

Ohr moved away from the garage door, jerked his head toward the main house, and held up a single finger when Jack walked toward the door. "Stop, Jack. Stay back here with us. If you go up to the front gate now, you might never come back."

Jack's hand froze on the door's brass knob. Its greasy window began rattling and vibrating to a loud, deep-throated rumble of motorcycles. Looking out the window, he saw a ragged army of motorcyclists speeding down toward the garage from both sides of the compound. They merged, rode back up to the front and circled around again, never stopping, roaring like a hundred thunderclaps. Backing away, Nassman and Ohr slid under the Mercedes. Jack dove to his right, pulling a black curtain along the wall to cover the half window.

The cadre of motorcycles revved their engines in an earthshaking roar. The first group drove from the left, between the house and a border of trees; the second roared from the right, between the house and the twenty-foot wall at the property's edge. Two men on each bike, they circled, bandoliers slung across their chests, rifles hanging on wide leather straps from their shoulders, and pistols in hand. The lines converged in front of the garage, passing each other in the courtyard. The riders pumped guns in the air, shouting, "Allahu Akbar!" Jack could not see the faces hidden behind the bandanas, but he could see the ferocity in their eyes.

"My God, Nassman, I've got to get to the girls. They must be terrified." He crouched below the window, bracing himself to pop up for another look. The continuous passing around both sides of the house presented a barrier that might as well have been a barbed wire fence.

"I have got to find a way through those crazy people. I'm going; cover me."

"No, you're not," Nassman yelled. "They're okay; Màasha's with them in the wine cellar. She knew this was coming. These guys are not interested in the girls. It's Khaki they've come for."

The motorcycles stopped circling and headed up the driveway toward the front of the compound.

"Those guys are revolutionary guards—militants. I know one of their leaders from school, so I called and told him that if they planned to question Khaki's loyalty to the ayatollah, they had to do it now, before he escaped to Istanbul with Ali," Ohr said.

Nassman planted his boot on a short stack of tires and from his Israeli bag of tricks pulled a Glock from a holster on his leg. "We're going in and getting Khaki's book before Ali finds Farideh."

A herd of motorcycles gathered at the front of the house, their engines idling as the riders' explosive shouts and chants grew louder. Men jumped off with the discipline of a riot and headed for the house. Heavy boots ground through the gravel, moving up marble stairs to the pompous front door, encouraged by the sound of gunshots slicing the air.

In the eye of the Islamist hurricane, Jack, Nassman, and Ohr saw an opportunity and charged out of the garage and across the courtyard to the back of the house. Jack wrapped a rag around his hand, broke the door's window, and unlatched the lock. He pulled glass shards out of his hand, squirting blood on the expensive floor. The bike brigade was concentrating on the front of the house, looking for their prey.

Racing up the stairs across the dining room's parquet floors, the three men ducked into the ransacked Qajar library. Nassman locked a firm hand on Jack's bicep. "Slow down," he said. "May be a few of them still in the house. Look; they killed one of Ali's guys."

The Turkish thug lay in a river of blood, one eye fixed open, the other eye splattered on his bushy mustache.

Jack moved the man's arm with his foot and kicked his Luger across the blood-soaked patterns of a masterpiece Sarouk carpet. He picked up the weapon and stuck it in his belt.

The men stopped at the sound of falsetto screams from the world's biggest arms dealer being hauled down his own marble steps. His terrified shrieks foretold the future he knew he would face.

From a corner window, they watched a trembling Khaki being lifted onto a Honda 750, his hands cuffed behind him. He was the rotten meat sandwiched between two burly, heavily bandoliered bikers. A dozen Suzuki, BMW, and Enfield bikes surrounded the Honda 750, roaring off into the Iranian dusk. Fumes from the motorcycles' cheap Persian petrol were still strong minutes after the revolutionary guards drove away. On the bottom steps, Jack spotted Khaki's black cashmere scarf caught on a bottom rail next to his cinnamon-red toupee, which was soaked like a wet rat.

Jack stepped over a dead bodyguard lying in the vestibule, where twin staircases curved and met on the second floor. The floor-to-ceiling windows faced Khaki's office. His throne-like chair caught blood dripping off his desk. His file drawers and bookcases had all been destroyed by the revolutionary guards. If their objective had been to wreck the room, then they had succeeded.

Jack raced across the landing and ran down the stairs, Ohr and Nassman on his heels.

Leah's sobbing stopped when they stepped into the wine cellar. He had to address her fears and keep moving. "Leah, your father will be okay. He'll be questioned and sent home in a couple of days." Jack didn't half believe it.

"You and Màasha are going to the airport. We're all going," Ohr said. "I'll drive the ambulance after we take care of some business."

Incredulous, Màasha followed them into the hall. Even with the household out of control, she did not panic. At the sight of Jack's bloody hand, her medical training took over. She examined his hand and tightened the handkerchief. "There's not enough room in the ambulance. How will you get out of Iran? Take my car; it has stickers from Shafa Hospital. Go there; they will give you a place to hide for now." Màasha's gray eyes began to well up.

Jack wanted to pick up the nurse and shake her like a piggy bank. "What the hell are you saying, Màasha? I'm getting pissed off. Where is Farideh? Is she joining Ali?"

"No, of course not. He took her; he had a gun. They went toward the back stairs, to Khaki's study. Farideh was crying, fighting to get away. I'm going back to Leah to finish getting her ready."

"Be careful, Màasha," said Ohr, placing his hand on her belly. "You've got our child to think about."

"Ali's got Farideh," Jack yelled.

"If he has Farideh, he has the ledger," said Nassman.

"Ali had help; the other bodyguard must have survived. We gotta find them," yelled Jack.

Ohr waved his pistol and yelled, "Ali knows the evacuation plan is ready, and he knows you're MI6, Jack. We can't leave until he's neutralized."

"There're a dozen places to hide in this house. Let's go. Farideh's rooms, third floor." Jack slipped in front of Nassman and Ohr, stopped, and held up his hand. "Wait. If Ali has Farideh, he could be holding a gun to her head. Be careful." Jack focused on both men and added, "Four years ago, you guys pulled off a rescue raid in Uganda, at Entebbe, in complete silence. Use that training now. Try her bedroom first."

Nassman chortled in an attempt to be funny. "Been there before, Jack?"

Jack answered with one finger, leading his two-man Israeli army up the stairs. Off the second landing, a narrow door led to the maid's entrance at the rear of Farideh's bedroom. Jack pointed to the door, waving the men forward to position themselves on either side of the doorframe. Jack reached for the knob, turned it, and heard it click. It was unlocked. He pushed it open silently, crouched, and saw Nassman and Ohr turn like commandos. One had his pistol high; the other held his at waist level.

They went through the princess-size closet, stopped, listened, and then moved toward the bedroom. Jack stepped carefully, Ohr silently behind him. The cold marble floor would amplify the thump of a cat's paw; desert boots would sound like Zildjian cymbals.

Ohr sidled past Jack through an anteroom door to a large dressing area. The darkness limited Jack's vision. Memory was of no use. He had never been in the dressing room or in Farideh's closet or anywhere else on the third floor.

A walk-around mahogany cabinet stood chest high in the closet's center, its stacked drawers accessible from either side. An armchair of gray suede with a matching footstool near a corner of the room was placed away from the wall so a maid could brush Farideh's hair. A salmon-colored merino wool carpet ran from the dressing room into the bedroom. Not a seam was visible; neither was the wire.

Jack was searching in the wardrobe when Ohr tripped on the wire, sprawling onto the carpet. Like lightning, a hand struck a sharp military blow to Ohr's neck. Before Jack could turn to help, he felt Ali's hands sliding under his arms and locking on the back of his neck. Jack dropped like a deadweight to his knees to break the hold. Ali spun away behind the cabinet, out of sight, below the beveled edge of the massive piece of furniture. His Turkish shouts for help were useless. Nassman had stunned the other Turk with the flat stub of his Glock, and Ohr finished him with a bullet in the Turk's hairy ear.

Jack rounded the cabinet as Ali jumped from a crouch and launched off the footstool to the top of the chest. Jack felt his blood vessels pounding at full velocity; he knew he would die if Ali was not neutralized immediately. Ali had pulled an ornamental, but lethal, scimitar off the wall, and whirled it, aiming at Jack's neck. He waited one second too long. Jack caught Ali's ankle and yanked him off his platform and onto the open drawer below.

With the kind of adrenaline shot that magnifies power in a fight to the death, Jack braced himself against the wall and slammed the heel of his boot hard on Ali's neck. The drawer's steel side rail sliced through Ali's neck, which was warm butter to the serrated metal. In a desperate movement, Ali brought his hands together to grasp the rail and pull it out. Blood spurted from his jugular, accompanying gurgling sounds that rose from deep in his throat in an oath only the devil would understand. His agate-black eyes showed the fear of death; he was losing his last fight.

"Where is Farideh?" Jack demanded.

Ali never heard the question.

For an instant, chaos morphed into an invisible stillness that crept over the two wrecked bodies. Death embraced the room with an aloneness Jack had never felt. Finality throbbed in his heart when he looked at the dead men.

"Farideh!" Jack yelled. No answer. He yelled again, running down the hallway, "Farideh!"

THIRTY-FOUR

Race to Mehrabad

A great sound roared up from the driveway like a drum corps accompanying a thunderstorm. It was the throaty adrenaline-pumping sound of another motorcycle starting up. Ohr ran to a window overlooking the courtyard and shouted, "Look; it's Farideh."

Jack saw the woman he loved straddling a BMW motorcycle, holding a leather briefcase against her chest with one hand and revving the engine with the other.

"Move!" commanded Ohr, rushing Nassman and Jack to the stairs.

The men burst into the courtyard as Màasha was finishing strapping Leah onto the gurney.

"Farideh, where were you? I couldn't find you," Jack said.

Farideh's red-rimmed eyes blinked with relief when she saw him. She was trembling when Jack flung his arms around her. "I'm so scared," she said, pointing to the leather satchel. "Ali knows I have my father's ledger, and he will kill me to get it. We need to leave now."

"Let's go, Ohr. Nassman, help Màasha," Jack shouted, wiping blood off his hands, pulling on a helmet.

Farideh reached to pull down dark goggles like a Saturday biker, except for the tears.

The bandana around Jack's bloody hand fell off when he snapped the chinstrap of the black helmet and mounted the motorcycle. His good hand motioned Farideh to anchor her feet on the bars beneath the hard saddle. She threw her arms around Jack, the briefcase wedged between them.

"We'll be at the airport in forty-five minutes!" Jack shouted. He looked over his shoulder at Farideh. She pushed her shield up, her moist brown eyes focused on him. "What happened up there, Jack? What did you do?"

"Farideh, Ali is gone."

"What do you mean? Where? When?"

"Ali is with his people."

Farideh pushed hard on Jack's back, screaming, "One of you killed him! I heard the fighting! I hate killing!" Her humanity overrode her hatred of Ali.

"It was going to be him or me."

She pounded his shoulders, screaming, "What has happened to my world? To my country?"

Since he had left London, Jack's self-respect had peaked and plummeted a dozen times. His improbable new life had changed everything he ever knew. Ali's death, no matter how ironic the manner, was the bottom. A thousand times in the three months since Hugh dragged him into a new life, he had asked himself what he was doing.

Farideh stopped her useless pummeling, gripped Jack's shoulder, and buried her head between his shoulder blades. She cried for her own life. The father she had loved as a child and the life she knew was gone—finished. All Iranians cried in their new reality; Iran would never be the same again—never.

Jack revved the motorcycle.

"You came back for me, for Leah. You've risked your life for us. Thank you."

Jack shrugged. "Hold the compliments until we get out of this sad country."

Leah was prostrate on the gurney. Màasha sat in the attendant seat, holding her hand, Nassman got up front. The ambulance began to roll; Ohr, at the wheel, edged up the driveway, drawing alongside the motorcycle. Nassman lowered his window, put on his most cherubic smile, and said, "Pass the briefcase to me. It'll be safer."

"Next year, in Jerusalem," Jack responded, pulling his goggles on. "I'll lead. Turn on the siren; stay with me." Jack revved the throttle, hit the kickstand with his heel, and charged up the driveway. The compound's gates, ripped apart by the Revolutionary Guard, lay partially open, one side hanging from a solitary hinge, allowing inches to spare. The ambulance slipped through.

Tehran's streets were jammed as usual with four-wheeled cars and trucks dodging four-legged burros weighed down with bulging sacks from the farm. Burros had no more respect for the ambulance siren than did cars. Shop tables along the city sidewalks gave the streets the appearance of a permanent bazaar. From massive posters covering windows of four- and five-story buildings, Ayatollah Khomeini watched everything and everyone.

The call to late-evening prayer was about to begin; merchants used it as a signal to close. One hawker stopped rewinding his puddled awning to look directly at the motorcycle and the ambulance. The man bowed his conical headdress, made the sign of a Yazidi, turned his gaze up to the heavens, and smiled. Jack grimaced behind his tinted face shield; there was little to smile about. Yazidis', Baha'is', and Zoroastrians' days were numbered in the land of revolutionary Islam.

The shrill siren pierced the continuing downpour, tormenting the tangled traffic. Ohr bounced through ruts, carving turns that dodged pedestrians with military skill. Lights reflected in the rain and fog like schools of sparkling red and silver sardines skimming through the surf. At the edge of town, the road to the airport narrowed. On alternating sides, staggered guard posts sheltered soldiers who sat, smoked, and kept out of the rain. If one of the soldiers shouted "Stop!" and was ignored, the trip to the airport would be over. A fusillade of bullets would riddle the ambulance.

Jack slowed, waving Ohr closer. "Keep going. Don't stop for any reason. We're halfway."

The six-wheel caravan sped past a trio of bandoliered Persian toughs holding machine guns, loitering in the shelter of the last downtown storefront. Pussycat revolutionaries did not like rain. The caravan ran alongside rippled rain gullies where city landscapes changed to low-rise apartment blocks, small neighborhood mosques, and shops whose feminine mannequins were draped in chadors. They passed the last decrepit merchant stalls and read a sign reading "Airport, thirteen kilometers."

The first ten kilometers went smoothly, and then Farideh shook Jack's shoulder, pointing to blue lights in the distance. Jack thumbed his helmet away from his ear, leaned back, and heard her say, "Roadblock. Could be police; could be Revolutionary Guard."

Jack calculated it was about a kilometer away. He inclined his head, raising his voice above the motorcycle's roar. "We can't stop; can't lose the time."

The flight crew would have begun their checklist by nine forty-five to have wheels up in plenty of time. The Red Crescent medical jet would not wait. General aviation takeoffs and landings were prohibited after ten at night.

Jack showed Farideh his watch.

He had rushed to catch flights out of Mehrabad a dozen times and knew there was only one route to the airport.

Jack's left hand shot over the top of his helmet, pointing right. Ohr got the message, saw a wide shoulder and bounced to a stop within sight of the guard post. Jack made a U-turn and wheeled in front of the ambulance, barely avoiding its door when Nassman jumped out, waving both hands. "We gotta get through that roadblock."

Farideh sat tight, her arms around the briefcase, while Jack rushed to the ambulance. Leah strained to see through the crescent etched on the window, trying to make sense of the unfolding chaos.

Ohr yelled out the window, "We can bust through. They'll think you're escorting the ambulance."

"Not happening," said Jack. "They'd shoot my tires or me."

Nassman shouted, "I'll take the bike."

"Farideh, bring the briefcase and get in up front next to Ohr. I'll squeeze under the gurney," said Jack.

Farideh dismounted and walked toward the ambulance. Nassman walked toward the motorcycle. When they passed, Nassman grabbed her in a half nelson, digging his nails into the back of her hand, ripping the briefcase loose. Farideh stumbled, lost her balance, and fell.

Jack was at her side in seconds.

"I'm okay. Get him."

Nassman was already on the motorcycle. He turned the bike in a semicircle and shouted, "Thanks, Jack." Waving the briefcase over his head, he yelled, "Tomorrow in Jerusalem." The motorcycle dug into the wet grassy berm, climbed up the bank off the shoulder, tires spitting mud and gravel, and roared into a field in the direction of Mehrabad Airport.

THIRTY-FIVE

Stop! Immigration!

Jack hustled his bruised and shaken girlfriend to the passenger seat of the ambulance. Màasha said something to Ohr in Hebrew and then turned her attention to Jack and ordered, "Get in. Ohr will get us out of this trap. He will get us through."

Jack dove under the gurney. Farideh removed her helmet, shivering in cold sweat.

Ohr raced off the graveled shoulder and back onto the road but got stuck behind a double-bottom truck. Even with the lights and siren rending the night, the truck driver would not give way. "Jack, hold on; I'll get through. Nassman will be at the plane with the briefcase, and we can deal with him there. He thinks we won't make it."

"You get us there, Ohr. I'll take care of Nassman."

Jack felt the ambulance jerk forward in the line of traffic, stop, and then jerk a few more feet. He wrapped his hands around the front rung under the gurney, pulling himself forward to see Farideh's profile—her high cheekbones, the curve of her shoulder. Seeing her filled him with courage.

Farideh sensed Jack looking at her. She put her arm over the seat back and mouthed, "I love you."

Closer to the checkpoint, the line of cars and trucks narrowed. Ohr's partial view was blocked by the double-bottom pushing into the left lane.

In an anxious tone, Farideh said, "Only two lanes open. Look, Ohr—a bypass on the side of the guardhouse." At the narrow opening between the embankment and the checkpoint, a guard slumped in his chair, napping under a Plexiglas overhang.

"The Farsi sign reads, 'Official Use Only'!" Farideh exclaimed.

"Go; we're official," Jack hollered.

Ohr flipped every emergency light switch he could find, put the siren in full blast mode and swerved right, into the "official" lane. On his left, the double-bottom lumbered toward a guard who signaled the driver that he did not need to stop. The driver slammed into a lower gear, blew his air horn, and groaned through.

In the few seconds it took for the guards to react to the ambulance making its own lane, Ohr shifted into second gear. "Jack, they will not come. They can see we're an ambulance."

Jack pulled himself up to the window, looked back, and said, "Forget that, Ohr; here they come."

Ohr flew past overloaded taxis crawling along under the wet burden of textile luggage strapped to the roof. He adjusted the siren, checked the emergency lights, and said, "I see them—two policemen on motorbikes. They'll either give us an escort or kill us." The furrows on his forehead wrinkled to the top of his bald head.

Jack caught on. "Ohr, you son of a bitch, you're enjoying this."

Màasha spoke up. "Nonsense. We went through their roadblock. If they catch up to us, we're dead. Or, if their stupid radios work, a fleet of motorcycles will be waiting at the passenger terminal."

Ohr whispered under his breath, "Mazel tov. We are not going to the passenger terminal. We're going to find Nassman."

"Ohr, Nassman was your friend, your partner. He should go to hell." Her voice quavered, hot with anger and cold with fear.

Ohr held up a flat palm. "You need to understand what Nassman is doing," he said, searching for gaps in the traffic.

"You're going to tell me he did it for us?"

"He did. From the moment we stopped, we were in trouble. We'll find him when we get to the airport. He'll have driven the motorcycle over ramps, railroad tracks—nothing will stop him from getting to the plane. He may want to deliver the folio to our guys. So what? We're all the same family. Stay down."

When the road narrowed on the luge-like airport ramp, Ohr saw an opening to get ahead of the double-bottom truck. He shot past, got directly in front of it, and then slammed hard on the brake pedal, tossing his unrestrained passengers around like stuffed dolls.

The truck driver's reaction was too late. He lost control of the twenty-two-wheel rig. On the slick pavement, the rear trailer broke off and whipsawed along the side rails, its momentum causing it to boomerang against the wall of the flyaway ramp. Metal tore against metal, and cargo crashed on the roadway in deafening crescendos of smashing crates. Hydraulic lines connecting the trailers hissed, steamed, and exploded in mushrooms of smoke and fire. The truck's driver was a sad second too late trying to jump from the cab that jackknifed over the guardrail, plunging into damnation.

Amid the fire and flying debris, one of the police motorcycles cartwheeled, following the truck over the side of the ramp.

"Where's the other one?" Ohr shouted.

"Saw him heading under the lorry," said Màasha, straining to see through the cataclysm, "He's gone."

Before the last scraps of metal landed on the road, Ohr was at a black mesh gate marked "GENERAL AVIATION." He skidded to a stop, screaming at a guard to raise the barrier. The bleary-eyed guard stuffed his head in the driver's window, yelled a litany of peasant epithets, and waved them through.

An immigration guard raised a flat palm. "You are for the medical jet? Follow me, quick. The commander will process your papers; everyone must go through immigration." He saw Leah's pale face and said, "The nurse can stay with the patient. Give me her papers." The guard's brusque manner was typical.

Farideh's heart pounded. "Jack, what should we do?"

"Just what he asks, and don't act like you know me. Ohr, take the ladies to the plane the moment they clear." Jack winked at Farideh and jumped out, ignoring the turmoil twisting in his mind.

"Stop," ordered the officer again, pushing Jack against the side of the ambulance. "The driver and the women stay in the car. You come with me."

"I'm not traveling," said Ohr. "I'll take them to the plane, then go back to Tehran. It is the English doctor who goes with them."

The officer measured Jack as they walked toward the immigration booth. "The airport closes in twenty minutes; so does my office. I hope we finish on time."

A portable heater warmed the lower half of a massive sergeant who took Jack's passport and read out the name "Bruce Chandler." He held the photo page of the passport next to Jack's face.

"Bruce Chandler? They called you Jack. It doesn't say you're a doctor. Explain."

"It's a nickname. Every British kid named Bruce has a nickname," said Jack. His imitation Yorkshire accent got lost as the officer's Farsi got louder. Jack caught a glimpse of Ohr driving slowly toward the Lockheed JetStar. It had the same Red Crescent markings as the ambulance.

When the sergeant finished flipping the pages of Jack's passport, he shook his head and pressed a button under his desk. A senior immigration officer rushed into the booth, barking orders to Jack and to the sergeant. The officer snatched the passport, pulled the sergeant out of his chair, swung the back of his hand at Jack, and plopped down.

"Now, let's have some order," he said in passable English. The lieutenant smoothed his uniform, looked at Jack's passport photo, then at Jack, and then looked back to the passport again, staring at Jack as if he were prey. Over his head, a clock showed only fifteen minutes until the airport closed. "We don't want you here. We don't want Americans."

Jack's blood went cold.

The lieutenant continued. "We don't want British or French or Canadians or any of you. You are all devils. You are all great Satans." He slapped Jack in the face with the passport, turned, and walked away.

Jack grabbed the passport and headed toward the plane, his heart a pounding jackhammer. His mission to get Farideh and Leah out of Iran was close to being accomplished. They were already on the small, fourteen-passenger medical evacuation plane. The objective of his other mission had last been seen in the hands of a focused, determined Mossad agent who also had to be on the plane.

The flashing red lights on the wing tips of the jet tossed luminescent red repetitions into the heavy mist. The pilots, bathed in a surreal glow of green navigation lights, finalizing preflight checks and squawking with the tower, were ready to go.

A two-step entry door unfolded from the plane to the tarmac. Dim interior cabin lights revealed little. In the misty darkness, a body rolled down the steps, squirming like a sidewinder snake, hands tied, legs trying to flip to a kneeling position. It was Nassman. Jack broke into a run when Farideh appeared at the door, struggling with the man who had thrown Nassman out. His arms wrapped around Farideh's waist, lifting her to the edge of the plane's doorway.

Jack screamed, "Hugh, stop! That's Farideh!"

"One more step, Jack, and she's dead." Hugh moved his arm up and around Farideh's neck. Her hands locked on his forearm, trying to pull loose. Hugh let go, pushed her back inside, reached the chain rail, and pulled up the airstair. The plane began to move.

Jack bent over Nassman and untied the French bowline, freeing his hands, yelling, "What's going on? We have to stop them."

"It's your guy, Jack. He has a buyer for the ledger."

The plane was two hundred feet down the taxiway, heading for the turn toward the active runway. Nassman spotted the ambulance first. "Ohr's going to intercept the plane."

"No, he isn't. He's coming at us."

The plane moved slowly, its navigation lights bouncing off the ambulance. "You fools, get in. Move!" Ohr shouted.

The ambulance's rear half-door popped open, and Nassman dove in. Jack was right behind him, sucking for air.

"Stay down. I'm going to block the plane."

"It can't be done," Jack said, "but do it anyway. A bullet in the back would be better than facing the butchers at Evin Prison."

The Lockheed's four engines hummed a cappella like four nuns in a choir. The pilot neared the intersection to turn off the taxiway and line up with the centerline lights on the active runway. Ohr sped along the right side of the taxiway, got ahead of the plane, and then whipped a left turn, stopping lengthwise in front of it. The plane's nose dipped over the forward strut, bounced, and bowed again, stopping within inches of the ambulance—close enough for Ohr to roll down his window and pat the plane on the nose.

Jack found the jet's door lever and yanked it open.

Hugh Ebanks filled the doorframe, both hands wrapped around the plastic-covered chain, grunting curses while trying to pull the door back up. "Screw off, Jack; your mission is done."

Jack jumped onto the bottom step, dodged a kick from Hugh, and grabbed his ankle, pulling him out of the plane. Hugh got to his feet, then body-slammed Jack to the ground. Jack delivered a hand chop to Hugh's neck and then rolled to his feet. Stunned by the force of the blow, Hugh struggled to get up. He recovered, then blocked an incoming punch with his left arm, landing his fist solidly in Jack's gut. Jack gasped for air, fell to the ground, and then swept his leg at Hugh, knocking him over. Jack grabbed a handful of Hugh's tight curls and bounced his adversary's head on the hard edge of the tarmac. "You lied, Ebanks. You had your own mission!" Jack punched Hugh in the face again, shouting, "I knew you had changed when we met in London!"

The engines could not drown out the rage Jack aimed at the man he was pounding senseless. He flipped him over, grabbing his arms for Nassman to wrap the rope Hugh had used on him minutes earlier. Nassman grinned as he cinched it tight.

Jack rolled Hugh over and had the turncoat's full attention. "Enjoy your life in Evin Prison."

Hugh's voice trembled in lower octaves of fear. He fixed his eyes on Jack and said, "Listen; I've always taken care of you, and I can make you rich. I got a guy who will give me two million bucks for the ledger. I'll cut you in for half."

Nassman wrenched Jack off Hugh in time to prevent another hammer blow. "Get his arms. We need to drag him away from the wheels. The Revolutionary Guard will make him talk, then kill him."

"Not happening, Nassman; we don't want him spilling his guts. We're putting him in the ambulance. Ohr can take it from there; you guys are good at that."

Trussed and eerily silent, the CIA's former Chief Intelligence Officer for the Middle East was thrown into the back of the ambulance like a sack of wet rags. Jack slammed the door. Ohr locked it and repeated his favorite saying: "Mazel tov."

THIRTY-SIX

MI6 vs. Mossad vs. CIA vs. Jack

T he ambulance's red lights still flickering, Ohr made a U-turn in the direction of the gate, and Jack and Nassman jumped onto the plane. Nassman pulled the door up, and Jack buckled into the front seat and shouted, "Let's go!"

The whine of the JetStar's engines resumed, and the pilot made a sharp turn onto the runway without waiting for clearance. The airport had closed, and the centerline lights had been switched off. Police cars and security vehicles, sirens screaming and horns honking, headed for the jet. Their sirens were drowned out by the roar of the JetStar's engines. They continued their futile race, running along both sides of the plane.

Jack watched the pilot push the throttles forward until the copilot said, "Airspeed alive, V1."

Halfway down the runway, Jack heard "Rotate," and the jet's nose lifted up into the rumbling dark clouds. The plane's wheels slammed into the well, and the lights of Tehran fell away. In the silence that always accompanies a takeoff, all the passengers had their own thoughts. They knew they would never see Iran again.

Double chimes signaled it was okay to smoke and take off seat belts, as if everything were normal. Jack raised an armrest to slide into the seat facing Farideh.

Her wet blouse stole Jack's eyes, if only for a second. Farideh's whimpers became sobs. Tears filled tissues held in clamshell grasps.

"Farideh, my darling, it's all right. We're okay now; we're together."

"This is the most tormented day of my life. I have been scared to death, thought you'd be arrested, then fighting … Who was that man? He knew you. Did you kill him too?" Farideh jumbled words and sobs, her eyes appealing for help. Her face fell into her hands.

"No, I didn't kill him." Jack's hand rested on her knee.

She shuddered. "What's happening now? Are we going to Istanbul?"

From the medical bed across the aisle, Leah turned her head toward Màasha, her brown eyes wide with anticipation, waiting to hear Jack's answer.

"Istanbul? No. We're going to London," interrupted Nassman, "but first we stop in Alexandria. We'll be met by my side, or Jack's. Both sides want this." He grinned, holding up Khaki's ledger. "So did Ebanks. Ohr will make sure he gets taken care of by some very interesting people." Nassman's poker face gave away nothing.

Farideh reached out for Jack's hand. She had not given up asking questions. "So who was that man? Why did he attack you? Are you a spy?"

"The man's name is Hugh Ebanks, and yes, he was a spy."

"You didn't answer."

"I'm not in the CIA."

"He's not in Mossad either," Nassman added.

The jet began to slow, and the PA system ticked on. "Seat belts, please. Going around a thunderstorm; expect turbulence."

Leah whimpered, "I don't like to fly."

Màasha strained against her belt. Her hands caressed Leah's temples as only a nurse can do, reassuring her, "We'll be all right." She unzipped a green medical bag embroidered with a white cross and took out a heavy blanket to cover Leah.

Nassman strapped into his seat in the first row.

Jack moved across the aisle to strap in behind Nassman. "You shoved Farideh too hard at the checkpoint."

"Sorry; action was needed, and it worked. You know how it goes. I have possession of the briefcase, so it goes to Tel Aviv, to Mossad, and then to Menachem Begin himself."

"Have you opened it?"

"Of course, and it's safe in this flight bag. It has what we expected, and the names of every buyer and seller in the Arab world, plus the IRA, Shining Path, and the PLO. Most of the handheld weapons are from the USSR—big stuff too. North Korea shows up; so does Pakistan. Khaki's minions kept details of every transaction: names, telex numbers, phones. He tied groups together. His dossier called him fastidious, and they were right.

"I noticed an interesting accounting entry about a fee he got for introducing the Pakistanis to train experts at Chanyeol Arms Plant in North Korea. With his Russian suppliers, Khaki could have gained control of Iran's entire weapons program. I read Farsi, Jack; we have the jackpot, as you'd call it. We'll turn our findings over to all the agencies—nothing to worry about. You'll get a copy. Now I'm going to sleep."

"Sweet dreams, my friend," said Jack. *It's not over.*

The plane wrestled out of the storm and into a clear night filled with sparkling stars. A slim yellow crescent moon visible on the western horizon matched the red crescent on the ambulance and the one on the airplane.

Jack turned back to Farideh. Her eyes still moist, she smiled at him, then rested her head on his shoulder.

"I'm going back to merchant banking to support our life together. I'm really sorry for what you have been through, but it's over now. I promise that from now on your life with me will be happy and you'll always be safe."

Farideh opened her arms to him in a fulfilling and promising embrace.

"This is Captain Ocalan speaking. We are out of Iranian airspace, now over Iraq. Touching down at El Nouzha Airport in Alexandria in three hours. The rest of the flight should be smooth."

"I'm going to rest a bit." Farideh leaned against her headrest and gazed out the window. The velocity of the events over the last few days had drained her. She was exhausted physically and emotionally, and she fell asleep before Jack reclined her seat. Since their chance meeting at the riding club, Farideh's lingering doubts about him had cleared up. In his determined and focused way, he made it clear that his love was real and, as he often said, forever. *We are truly meant for each other.*

Nassman lay sleeping on the floor, his snoring louder than the noise from the engines.

The plane descended to land at El Nouzha, where a pickup truck with flashing yellow lights waited. The pickup got in front of the plane and flipped on the lights of a wide roof-mounted reader board flashing "FOLLOW ME."

Captain Ocalan shut down the engines in front of a military hangar, stepped out of the cockpit, and announced, "Wait here, please. The authorities must see our papers and clear the plane. We'll be right back." Both pilots headed toward the sand-colored office, dossiers in hand.

A few feet away, a black official car caught Jack's attention. Its driver waited until the pilots passed and then opened the back door for a tall, slender man who walked directly up the steps into the plane. He spotted Nassman first, removed a black glove, extended his hand like a politician, and said, "Hello, I'm Algernon Trivelpiece. You are Mr. Nassman?"

"I am."

Trivelpiece nodded. "Yes, I've heard a lot about you. The Red Crescent told Tel Aviv you'd be on the plane."

Nassman grinned. "And I know who you are, Mr. Trivelpiece. You've got a good man here."

Trivelpiece glanced at Jack. "Oh, yes, of course. You must be Mr. Devlin, the young lady's boyfriend." The chief placed his hand firmly on Jack's shoulder for a moment and then moved past him toward the ladies, introducing himself with proper upper-class courtesy. "Ladies, I'm from the British government, here to welcome you. I expect the last few days have not been easy, but you are safe with us now. You'll be well taken care of." He pointed out the window to a Falcon jet with markings of the British High Commission. "That plane will take you on to London, where arrangements have been made at Hammersmith Hospital. Mr. Devlin will accompany you—won't you, Mr. Devlin?" His smile, when he looked at Leah, was as long as he was tall. "Can you walk, miss?"

"She must conserve her strength, Mr. Trivelpiece. We will use the gurney," said Màasha.

Leah motioned Jack to her side and said, "Jack, I'll be all right now. Farideh has told me the incredible news. We're a match, and she is donating one of her kidneys to me. She said you made the arrangements."

Jack took her hand and said, "It wouldn't have happened without Màasha, Nassman, and Ohr. They were the key people."

Leah got the final word. "Farideh loves you, Jack. Take care of her."

"My assistant, Pandora Quince, will be waiting for you at Heathrow Airport," said Trivelpiece.

"Sorry, everyone; we have to get on the plane," the British medic interrupted. "Wheels up in twenty minutes. The ladies and you, sir"—he pointed to Jack—"disembark please, and go over to the Falcon jet."

Trivelpiece laid his folio briefcase on the row in front of Nassman and said, "May we have a word, please, Mr. Nassman? Privately, if you don't mind—out of the way of these fine young people." The chief nodded to Jack, used a shoulder shrug to indicate his briefcase on the seat, and walked to the back of the plane. Nassman followed, carrying the ledger.

Jack returned Trivelpiece's nod, waited a few seconds, winked at Farideh, and then slid the silver clasp off the chief's briefcase. It contained a slightly smaller duplicate briefcase that held a thick file, the size of the ledger.

The conversation from the rear of the plane modulated after a few minutes, and in a loud voice Trivelpiece ordered, "Mr. Devlin, my briefcase, sir—would you bring it to me?" Trivelpiece moved halfway toward the front of the plane. "You see, Mr. Devlin, we have gotten on quite well. Mr. Nassman and I are going to be driven into Cairo to put this ledger into safe hands at his embassy." The chief turned away from Jack and said, "Mr. Nassman, kindly put the ledger in the briefcase. Jack, lock it, please, give the key to Mr. Nassman, and follow us with the briefcase."

"Yes, sir."

Trivelpiece gestured like a matador, directing Nassman to the door. They quickly descended the steps with Jack right behind them.

Jack shook hands with the chief, then gave Nassman the briefcase and a side hug.

"You're a good man, Agent Devlin. We will meet again," said Nassman.

From the plane's doorway, Farideh tossed a cheerio to the chief and a mazel tov to Nassman.

Jack walked back up the steps and said, "Farideh, wait a moment; I forgot something."

When they stepped off the Red Crescent plane, he took Farideh's hand. As they walked across the tarmac, Jack felt like a kid again. It was the first time they had held hands in public.

On the Falcon, Màasha took over from the medics, tucked Leah in, fastened a seat belt over her blanket, and fluffed her pillow. The Scottish-accented pilot's voice instructed everyone to "Buckle up, lads and lassies," and the Falcon rocketed into the western sky.

Farideh looked puzzled when Jack kicked a green medical bag under the seat in front of him. "Why do you have Màasha's supply bag?"

"It has a couple of things I found while everyone was sleeping."

"What's in the bag? I want to see."

Jack shrugged, stuck his toe under the duffel's strap, and dragged it toward him. Farideh leaned closer to watch Jack pull out a black briefcase, put his thumb and forefinger on the clasp, and pop it open. He felt the quick tremor of a chill pass through Farideh's body.

"Oh my God, Jack. You got it. You got the ledger!"

He grinned. "Intact; and in a few days MI6 will identify every dirty scumbag involved. This ledger was not the objective; it was the leverage. It was the leverage that got me into Iran to get you out."

With a sparkle in her eye, she looked at him and said, "Now we can be together, forever. You completed your mission—the only mission that ever mattered. I love you."

An *Improbable Spy* is a work of fiction with significant basis in historical fact. The longest hostage crisis in history began in the American embassy in Tehran on November 4, 1979, and ended fourteen-and-a-half months later. The author was in Tehran when the hostages were taken, and he escaped the following week. He had a business relationship with a well-placed Iranian banker whose daughter suffered from kidney disease. Under the banker's protection, the author succeeded in returning to Tehran to arrange her extraction. He later learned she had a successful kidney transplant in London. He never saw her again.

On April 24, 1980, in a poorly planned attempt to rescue the fifty-three hostages, President Jimmy Carter launched Operation Eagle's Claw. The mission landed in Khorasan Province and failed, costing the lives of eight American soldiers and one Iranian civilian. On April 26, yielding to Russian advice, Iran separated the hostages and scattered them around the country. When Ronald Reagan took the oath of office as the fortieth president of the United States on January 20, 1981, the hostages were released. The actionable information from the KGB defector led to his exfiltration to the US, where he lived under protected cover in Texas.

If asked, MI6 and the CIA would deny ever having had any association with the author.

If asked, the author would deny ever having had any association with MI6 or the CIA.

ACKNOWLEDGMENTS

My deepest thanks to Jennifer Stewart, who deciphered my terrible handwriting while editing, cajoling, and coaching as we reworked every draft. Her gifts in narrowing lengthy descriptions, suggesting a word here, or deleting an entire paragraph there were done with humor, focus, and occasionally, kindness. Were I a better writer, I could come up with some magnificent words, but "thank you, Jennifer" says it best. Jennifer made the really improbable happen.

For their friendship and wisdom, I also want to thank Bill Adams, Tim Barker, Julian Beale, Darlene Brice, Lanny Broders, John Evans, John Fox, Deborah Gaal, Raya Jaffee, Jody Killion, Louella Nelson, Dr. Madeline Pahl, and Judy Whitmore, who read drafts, gave feedback, and helped with fact-checking. Without their help, there would not be a book.

CPSIA information can be obtained
at www.ICGtesting.com
Printed in the USA
BVHW032141300120
571072BV00001B/8

9 781532 080104